THE MYSTERY OF CHOICE

THE MYSTERY OF CHOICE

By
ROBERT WILLIAM CHAMBERS

Short Story Index Reprint Series

BOOKS FOR LIBRARIES PRESS
FREEPORT, NEW YORK

First Published 1897
Reprinted 1969

STANDARD BOOK NUMBER:
8369-3089-4

LIBRARY OF CONGRESS CATALOG CARD NUMBER:
73-94710

MANUFACTURED
BY
HALLMARK LITHOGRAPHERS, INC.
IN THE U.S.A.

DEDICATION.

There is a maid, demure as she is wise,
With all of April in her winsome eyes,
And to my tales she listens pensively,
With slender fingers clasped about her knee,
Watching the sparrows on the balcony.

Shy eyes that, lifted up to me,
Free all my heart of vanity;
Clear eyes, that speak all silently,
Sweet as the silence of a nunnery—
Read, for I write my rede for you alone,
Here where the city's mighty monotone
Deepens the silence to a symphony—
Silence of Saints, and Seers, and Sorcery.

Arms and the Man!   A noble theme, I ween!
Alas! I can not sing of these, Eileen—
Only of maids and men and meadow-grass,
Of sea and fields and woodlands, where I pass;
Nothing but these I know, Eileen, alas!

Clear eyes that, lifted up to me,
Free all my soul from vanity;
Gray eyes, that speak all wistfully—
Nothing but these I know, alas!

R. W. C.

April, 1896.

v

INTRODUCTION.

I.

Where two fair paths, deep flowered
          And leaf-embowered,
Creep East and West across a World concealed,
Which shall he take who journeys far afield ?

II.

Canst thou then say, "I go,"
          Or "I forego" ?
What turns thee East or West, as thistles blow ?
Is fair more fair than fair—and dost thou know ?

III.

Turn to the West, unblessed
          And uncaressed ;
Turn to the East, and, seated at the Feast
Thou shalt find Life, or Death from Life released.

IV.

And thou who lovest best
          A maid dark-tressed,
And passest others by with careless eye,
Canst thou tell why thou choosest ? Tell, then ; why ?

V.

So when thy kiss is given
          Or half-forgiven,
Why should she tremble, with her face flame-hot,
Or laugh and whisper, "Love, I tremble not" ?

VI.

Or when thy hand may catch
        A half-drawn latch,
What draws thee from the door, to turn and pass
Through streets unknown, dim, still, and choked with
        grass ?

VII.

What !   Canst thou not foresee
        The Mystery ?
Heed !   For a Voice commands thy every deed !
And it hath sounded.   And thou needs must heed !

                                        R. W. C.

    1896.

CONTENTS.

ix

THE PURPLE EMPEROR.

THE PURPLE EMPEROR.

Un souvenir heureux est peut-être, sur terre,
Plus vrai que le bonheur.
                    A. DE MUSSET.

I.

THE Purple Emperor watched me in silence.
I cast again, spinning out six feet more of waterproof silk, and, as the line hissed through the air
far across the pool, I saw my three flies fall on
the water like drifting thistledown. The Purple Emperor sneered.

"You see," he said, "I am right. There is
not a trout in Brittany that will rise to a tailed
fly."

"They do in America," I replied.

"Zut! for America!" observed the Purple
Emperor.

"And trout take a tailed fly in England," I
insisted sharply.

"Now do I care what things or people do in
England?" demanded the Purple Emperor.

"You don't care for anything except yourself and your wriggling caterpillars," I said,
more annoyed than I had yet been.

3

The Purple Emperor sniffed. His broad, hairless, sunburnt features bore that obstinate expression which always irritated me. Perhaps the manner in which he wore his hat intensified the irritation, for the flapping brim rested on both ears, and the two little velvet ribbons which hung from the silver buckle in front wiggled and fluttered with every trivial breeze. His cunning eyes and sharp-pointed nose were out of all keeping with his fat red face. When he met my eye, he chuckled.

"I know more about insects than any man in Morbihan—or Finistère either, for that matter," he said.

"The Red Admiral knows as much as you do," I retorted.

"He doesn't," replied the Purple Emperor angrily.

"And his collection of butterflies is twice as large as yours," I added, moving down the stream to a spot directly opposite him.

"It is, is it?" sneered the Purple Emperor. "Well, let me tell you, Monsieur Darrel, in all his collection he hasn't a specimen, a single specimen, of that magnificent butterfly, Apatura Iris, commonly known as the 'Purple Emperor.'"

"Everybody in Brittany knows that," I said, casting across the sparkling water; "but just because you happen to be the only man who ever captured a 'Purple Emperor' in

Morbihan, it doesn't follow that you are an authority on sea-trout flies. Why do you say that a Breton sea-trout won't touch a tailed fly?"

"It's so," he replied.

"Why? There are plenty of May-flies about the stream."

"Let 'em fly!" snarled the Purple Emperor, "you won't see a trout touch 'em."

My arm was aching, but I grasped my split bamboo more firmly, and, half turning, waded out into the stream and began to whip the ripples at the head of the pool. A great green dragon-fly came drifting by on the summer breeze and hung a moment above the pool, glittering like an emerald.

"There's a chance! Where is your butterfly net?" I called across the stream.

"What for? That dragon-fly? I've got dozens—Anax Junius, Drury, characteristic, anal angle of posterior wings, in male, round; thorax marked with——"

"That will do," I said fiercely. "Can't I point out an insect in the air without this burst of erudition? Can you tell me, in simple everyday French, what this little fly is—this one, flitting over the eel grass here beside me? See, it has fallen on the water."

"Huh!" sneered the Purple Emperor, "that's a Linnobia annulus."

"What's that?" I demanded.

Before he could answer there came a heavy splash in the pool, and the fly disappeared.

"He! he! he!" tittered the Purple Emperor. "Didn't I tell you the fish knew their business? That was a sea-trout. I hope you don't get him."

He gathered up his butterfly net, collecting box, chloroform bottle, and cyanide jar. Then he rose, swung the box over his shoulder, stuffed the poison bottles into the pockets of his silver-buttoned velvet coat, and lighted his pipe. This latter operation was a demoralizing spectacle, for the Purple Emperor, like all Breton peasants, smoked one of those microscopical Breton pipes which requires ten minutes to find, ten minutes to fill, ten minutes to light, and ten seconds to finish. With true Breton stolidity he went through this solemn rite, blew three puffs of smoke into the air, scratched his pointed nose reflectively, and waddled away, calling back an ironical "Au revoir, and bad luck to all Yankees!"

I watched him out of sight, thinking sadly of the young girl whose life he made a hell upon earth—Lys Trevec, his niece. She never admitted it, but we all knew what the black-and-blue marks meant on her soft, round arm, and it made me sick to see the look of fear come into her eyes when the Purple Emperor waddled into the café of the Groix Inn.

It was commonly said that he half-starved

her. This she denied. Marie Joseph and 'Fine
Lelocard had seen him strike her the day after
the Pardon of the Birds because she had liber-
ated three bullfinches which he had limed the
day before. I asked Lys if this were true, and
she refused to speak to me for the rest of the
week. There was nothing to do about it. If
the Purple Emperor had not been avaricious, I
should never have seen Lys at all, but he could
not resist the thirty francs a week which I offered him; and Lys posed for me all day long,
happy as a linnet in a pink thorn hedge. Never-
theless, the Purple Emperor hated me, and con-
stantly threatened to send Lys back to her dreary
flax-spinning. He was suspicious, too, and when
he had gulped down the single glass of cider
which proves fatal to the sobriety of most Bretons, he would pound the long, discoloured
oaken table and roar curses on me, on Yves Terrec, and on the Red Admiral. We were the
three objects in the world which he most hated:
me, because I was a foreigner, and didn't care
a rap for him and his butterflies; and the Red
Admiral, because he was a rival entomologist.

He had other reasons for hating Terrec.

The Red Admiral, a little wizened wretch,
with a badly adjusted glass eye and a passion for
brandy, took his name from a butterfly which
predominated in his collection. This butterfly, commonly known to amateurs as the "Red
Admiral," and to entomologists as Vanessa Ata-

lanta, had been the occasion of scandal among the entomologists of France and Brittany. For the Red Admiral had taken one of these common insects, dyed it a brilliant yellow by the aid of chemicals, and palmed it off on a credulous collector as a South African species, absolutely unique. The fifty francs which he gained by this rascality were, however, absorbed in a suit for damages brought by the outraged amateur a month later; and when he had sat in the Quimperlé jail for a month, he reappeared in the little village of St. Gildas soured, thirsty, and burning for revenge. Of course we named him the Red Admiral, and he accepted the name with suppressed fury.

The Purple Emperor, on the other hand, had gained his imperial title legitimately, for it was an undisputed fact that the only specimen of that beautiful butterfly, Apatura Iris, or the Purple Emperor, as it is called by amateurs—the only specimen that had ever been taken in Finistère or in Morbihan—was captured and brought home alive by Joseph Marie Gloanec, ever afterward to be known as the Purple Emperor.

When the capture of this rare butterfly became known the Red Admiral nearly went crazy. Every day for a week he trotted over to the Groix Inn, where the Purple Emperor lived with his niece, and brought his microscope to bear on the rare newly captured butterfly, in hopes of detecting a fraud. But this specimen was genuine, and he leered through his microscope in vain.

"No chemicals there, Admiral," grinned the Purple Emperor; and the Red Admiral chattered with rage.

To the scientific world of Brittany and France the capture of an Apatura Iris in Morbihan was of great importance. The Museum of Quimper offered to purchase the butterfly, but the Purple Emperor, though a hoarder of gold, was a monomaniac on butterflies, and he jeered at the Curator of the Museum. From all parts of Brittany and France letters of inquiry and congratulation poured in upon him. The French Academy of Sciences awarded him a prize, and the Paris Entomological Society made him an honorary member. Being a Breton peasant, and a more than commonly pig-headed one at that, these honours did not disturb his equanimity; but when the little hamlet of St. Gildas elected him mayor, and, as is the custom in Brittany under such circumstances, he left his thatched house to take up an official life in the little Groix Inn, his head became completely turned. To be mayor in a village of nearly one hundred and fifty people! It was an empire! So he became unbearable, drinking himself viciously drunk every night of his life, maltreating his niece, Lys Trevec, like the barbarous old wretch that he was, and driving the Red Admiral nearly frantic with his eternal harping on

the capture of Apatura Iris. Of course he refused to tell where he had caught the butterfly.
The Red Admiral stalked his footsteps, but
in vain.

"He! he! he!" nagged the Purple Emper-
or, cuddling his chin over a glass of cider;
"I saw you sneaking about the St. Gildas
spinny yesterday morning. So you think you
can find another Apatura Iris by running after
me? It won't do, Admiral, it won't do, d'ye
see?"

The Red Admiral turned yellow with mortification and envy, but the next day he actually
took to his bed, for the Purple Emperor had
brought home not a butterfly but a live chrysalis, which, if successfully hatched, would become a perfect specimen of the invaluable Apatura Iris. This was the last straw. The Red
Admiral shut himself up in his little stone cottage, and for weeks now he had been invisible
to everybody except 'Fine Lelocard who carried
him a loaf of bread and a mullet or langouste
every morning.

The withdrawal of the Red Admiral from the
society of St. Gildas excited first the derision
and finally the suspicion of the Purple Emperor.
What deviltry could he be hatching? Was he
experimenting with chemicals again, or was he
engaged in some deeper plot, the object of which
was to discredit the Purple Emperor? Roux,
the postman, who carried the mail on foot once

a day from Bannalec, a distance of fifteen miles each way, had brought several suspicious letters, bearing English stamps, to the Red Admiral, and the next day the Admiral had been observed at his window grinning up into the sky and rubbing his hands together. A night or two after this apparition the postman left two packages at the Groix Inn for a moment while he ran across the way to drink a glass of cider with me. The Purple Emperor, who was roaming about the café, snooping into everything that did not concern him, came upon the packages and examined the postmarks and addresses. One of the packages was square and heavy, and felt like a book. The other was also square, but very light, and felt like a pasteboard box. They were both addressed to the Red Admiral, and they bore English stamps.

When Roux, the postman, came back, the Purple Emperor tried to pump him, but the poor little postman knew nothing about the contents of the packages, and after he had taken them around the corner to the cottage of the Red Admiral the Purple Emperor ordered a glass of cider, and deliberately fuddled himself until Lys came in and tearfully supported him to his room. Here he became so abusive and brutal that Lys called to me, and I went and settled the trouble without wasting any words. This also the Purple Emperor remembered, and waited his chance to get even with me.

That had happened a week ago, and until to-day he had not deigned to speak to me.

Lys had posed for me all the week, and to-day being Saturday, and I lazy, we had decided to take a little relaxation, she to visit and gossip with her little black-eyed friend Yvette in the neighbouring hamlet of St. Julien, and I to try the appetites of the Breton trout with the contents of my American fly book.

I had thrashed the stream very conscientiously for three hours, but not a trout had risen to my cast, and I was piqued. I had begun to believe that there were no trout in the St. Gildas stream, and would probably have given up had I not seen the sea trout snap the little fly which the Purple Emperor had named so scientifically. That set me thinking. Probably the Purple Emperor was right, for he certainly was an expert in everything that crawled and wriggled in Brittany. So I matched, from my American fly book, the fly that the sea trout had snapped up, and withdrawing the cast of three, knotted a new leader to the silk and slipped a fly on the loop. It was a queer fly. It was one of those unnameable experiments which fascinate anglers in sporting stores and which generally prove utterly useless. Moreover, it was a tailed fly, but of course I easily remedied that with a stroke of my penknife. Then I was all ready, and I stepped out into the hurrying rapids and cast straight as an arrow to the spot

where the sea trout had risen. Lightly as a
plume the fly settled on the bosom of the pool;
then came a startling splash, a gleam of silver,
and the line tightened from the vibrating rod-
tip to the shrieking reel. Almost instantly I
checked the fish, and as he floundered for a moment, making the water boil along his glittering
sides, I sprang to the bank again, for I saw that
the fish was a heavy one and I should probably
be in for a long run down the stream. The five-
ounce rod swept in a splendid circle, quivering
under the strain. " Oh, for a gaff-hook! " I
cried aloud, for I was now firmly convinced that
I had a salmon to deal with, and no sea trout
at all.

Then as I stood, bringing every ounce to
bear on the sulking fish, a lithe, slender girl
came hurriedly along the opposite bank calling
out to me by name.

" Why, Lys! " I said, glaneing up for a second, " I thought you were at St. Julien with
Yvette."

" Yvette has gone to Bannelec. I went
home and found an awful fight going on at the
Groix Inn, and I was so frightened that I came
to tell you."

The fish dashed off at that moment, carrying all the line my reel held, and I was compelled
to follow him at a jump. Lys, active and graceful as a young deer, in spite of her Pont-Aven
sabots, followed along the opposite bank until

the fish settled in a deep pool, shook the line savagely once or twice, and then relapsed into the sulks.

"Fight at the Groix Inn?" I called across the water. "What fight?"

"Not exactly fight," quavered Lys, "but the Red Admiral has come out of his house at last, and he and my uncle are drinking together and disputing about butterflies. I never saw my uncle so angry, and the Red Admiral is sneering and grinning. Oh, it is almost wicked to see such a face!"

"But Lys," I said, scarcely able to repress a smile, "your uncle and the Red Admiral are always quarrelling and drinking."

"I know—oh, dear me!—but this is different, Monsieur Darrel. The Red Admiral has grown old and fierce since he shut himself up three weeks ago, and—oh, dear! I never saw such a look in my uncle's eyes before. He seemed insane with fury. His eyes—I can't speak of it—and then Terrec came in."

"Oh," I said more gravely, "that was unfortunate. What did the Red Admiral say to his son?"

Lys sat down on a rock among the ferns, and gave me a mutinous glance from her blue eyes.

Yves Terrec, loafer, poacher, and son of Louis Jean Terrec, otherwise the Red Admiral, had been kicked out by his father, and had also been forbidden the village by the Purple Emperor, in his majestic capacity of mayor. Twice the young ruffian had returned: once to rifle the bedroom of the Purple Emperor—an unsuccessful enterprise—and another time to rob his own father. He succeeded in the latter attempt, but was never caught, although he was frequently seen roving about the forests and moors with his gun. He openly menaced the Purple Emperor; vowed that he would marry Lys in spite of all the gendarmes in Quimperlé; and these same gendarmes he led many a long chase through brier-filled swamps and over miles of yellow gorse.

What he did to the Purple Emperor—what he intended to do—disquieted me but little; but I worried over his threat concerning Lys. During the last three months this had bothered me a great deal; for when Lys came to St. Gildas from the convent the first thing she captured was my heart. For a long time I had refused to believe that any tie of blood linked this dainty blue-eyed creature with the Purple Emperor. Although she dressed in the velvet-laced bodice and blue petticoat of Finistère, and wore the bewitching white coiffe of St. Gildas, it seemed like a pretty masquerade. To me she was as sweet and as gently bred as many a maiden of the noble Faubourg who danced with her cousins at a Louis XV fête champêtre. So when Lys said that Yves Terrec had returned

openly to St. Gildas, I felt that I had better be
there also.

"What did Terrec say, Lys?" I asked,
watching the line vibrating above the placid
pool.

The wild rose colour crept into her cheeks.
"Oh," she answered, with a little toss of her
chin, "you know what he always says."

"That he will carry you away?"

"Yes."

"In spite of the Purple Emperor, the Red
Admiral, and the gendarmes?"

"Yes."

"And what do you say, Lys?"

"I?   Oh, nothing."

"Then let me say it for you."

Lys looked at her delicate pointed sabots,
the sabots from Pont-Aven, made to order.
They fitted her little foot.   They were her only
luxury.

"Will you let me answer for you, Lys?" I
asked.

"You, Monsieur Darrel?"

"Yes.   Will you let me give him his answer?"

"Mon Dieu, why should you concern yourself, Monsieur Darrel?"

The fish lay very quiet, but the rod in my
hand trembled.

"Because I love you, Lys."

The wild rose colour in her cheeks deepened;

she gave a gentle gasp, then hid her curly head in her hands.

"I love you, Lys."

"Do you know what you say?" she stammered.

"Yes, I love you."

She raised her sweet face and looked at me across the pool.

"I love you," she said, while the tears stood like stars in her eyes. "Shall I come over the brook to you?"

II.

That night Yves Terrec left the village of St. Gildas vowing vengeance against his father, who refused him shelter.

I can see him now, standing in the road, his bare legs rising like pillars of bronze from his straw-stuffed sabots, his short velvet jacket torn and soiled by exposure and dissipation, and his eyes, fierce, roving, bloodshot—while the Red Admiral squeaked curses on him, and hobbled away into his little stone cottage.

"I will not forget you!" cried Yves Terrec, and stretched out his hand toward his father with a terrible gesture. Then he whipped his gun to his cheek and took a short step forward, but I caught him by the throat before he could fire, and a second later we were rolling in the dust of the Bannalec road. I had to hit him a heavy blow behind the ear before he would let go, and then, rising and shaking myself, I dashed his muzzle-loading fowling piece to bits against a wall, and threw his knife into the river. The Purple Emperor was looking on with a queer light in his eyes. It was plain that he was sorry Terrec had not choked me to death.

"He would have killed his father," I said, as I passed him, going toward the Groix Inn.

"That's his business," snarled the Purple Emperor. There was a deadly light in his eyes. For a moment I thought he was going to attack me; but he was merely viciously drunk, so I shoved him out of my way and went to bed, tired and disgusted.

The worst of it was I couldn't sleep, for I feared that the Purple Emperor might begin to abuse Lys. I lay restlessly tossing among the sheets until I could stay there no longer. I did not dress entirely; I merely slipped on a pair of chaussons and sabots, a pair of knickerbockers, a jersey, and a cap. Then, loosely tying a handkerchief about my throat, I went down the worm-eaten stairs and out into the moonlit road. There was a candle flaring in the Purple Emperor's window, but I could not see him.

"He's probably dead drunk," I thought, and looked up at the window where, three years before, I had first seen Lys.

"Asleep, thank Heaven!" I muttered, and wandered out along the road. Passing the small cottage of the Red Admiral, I saw that it was dark, but the door was open. I stepped inside the hedge to shut it, thinking, in case Yves Terrec should be roving about, his father would lose whatever he had left.

Then, after fastening the door with a stone, I wandered on through the dazzling Breton moonlight. A nightingale was singing in a willow swamp below, and from the edge of the mere, among the tall swamp grasses, myriads of frogs chanted a bass chorus.

When I returned, the eastern sky was beginning to lighten, and across the meadows on the cliffs, outlined against the paling horizon, I saw a seaweed gatherer going to his work among the curling breakers on the coast. His long rake was balanced on his shoulder, and the sea wind carried his song across the meadows to me:

> St. Gildas!
> St. Gildas!
> Pray for us,
> Shelter us,
> Us who toil in the sea.

Passing the shrine at the entrance of the village, I took off my cap and knelt in prayer to Our Lady of Faöuet; and if I neglected myself in that prayer, surely I believed Our Lady of Faöuet would be kinder to Lys. It is said that the shrine casts white shadows. I looked, but saw only the moonlight. Then very peacefully I went to bed again, and was only awakened by the clank of sabres and the trample of horses in the road below my window.

"Good gracious!" I thought, "it must be eleven o'clock, for there are the gendarmes from Quimperlé."

I looked at my watch; it was only half-past eight, and as the gendarmes made their rounds every Thursday at eleven, I wondered what had brought them out so early to St. Gildas.

"Of course," I grumbled, rubbing my eyes, "they are after Terrec," and I jumped into my limited bath.

Before I was completely dressed I heard a timid knock, and opening my door, razor in hand, stood astonished and silent. Lys, her blue eyes wide with terror, leaned on the threshold.

"My darling!" I cried, "what on earth is the matter?" But she only clung to me, panting like a wounded sea gull. At last, when I drew her into the room and raised her face to mine, she spoke in a heart-breaking voice:

"Oh, Dick! they are going to arrest you, but I will die before I believe one word of what they say. No, don't ask me," and she began to sob desperately.

When I found that something really serious was the matter, I flung on my coat and cap, and, slipping one arm about her waist, went down the stairs and out into the road. Four gendarmes sat on their horses in front of the café door; beyond them, the entire population of St. Gildas gaped, ten deep.

"Hello, Durand!" I said to the brigadier, "what the devil is this I hear about arresting me?"

"It's true, mon ami," replied Durand with sepulchral sympathy. I looked him over from the tip of his spurred boots to his sulphur-yellow sabre belt, then upward, button by button, to his disconcerted face.

"What for?" I said scornfully. "Don't try any cheap sleuth work on me! Speak up, man, what's the trouble?"

The Purple Emperor, who sat in the doorway staring at me, started to speak, but thought better of it and got up and went into the house. The gendarmes rolled their eyes mysteriously and looked wise.

"Come, Durand," I said impatiently, "what's the charge?"

"Murder," he said in a faint voice.

"What!" I cried incredulously. "Nonsense! Do I look like a murderer? Get off your horse, you stupid, and tell me who's murdered."

Durand got down, looking very silly, and came up to me, offering his hand with a propitiatory grin.

"It was the Purple Emperor who denounced you! See, they found your handkerchief at his door——"

"Whose door, for Heaven's sake?" I cried.

"Why, the Red Admiral's!"

"The Red Admiral's? What has he done?"

"Nothing—he's only been murdered."

I could scarcely believe my senses, although they took me over to the little stone cottage and pointed out the blood-spattered room. But the horror of the thing was that the corpse of the murdered man had disappeared, and there only remained a nauseating lake of blood on the stone floor, in the centre of which lay a human hand. There was no doubt as to whom the hand belonged, for everybody who had ever seen the Red Admiral knew that the shrivelled bit of flesh which lay in the thickening blood was the hand of the Red Admiral. To me it looked like the severed claw of some gigantic bird.

"Well," I said, "there's been murder committed. Why don't you do something?"

"What?" asked Durand.

"I don't know. Send for the Commissaire."

"He's at Quimperlé. I telegraphed."

"Then send for a doctor, and find out how long this blood has been coagulating."

"The chemist from Quimperlé is here; he's a doctor."

"What does he say?"

"He says that he doesn't know."

"And who are you going to arrest?" I inquired, turning away from the spectacle on the floor.

"I don't know," said the brigadier solemnly; "you are denounced by the Purple Emperor, because he found your handkerchief at the door when he went out this morning."

"Just like a pig-headed Breton!" I exclaimed, thoroughly angry. "Did he not mention Yves Terrec?"

"No."

"Of course not," I said. "He overlooked the fact that Terrec tried to shoot his father last night, and that I took away his gun. All that counts for nothing when he finds my handkerchief at the murdered man's door."

"Come into the café," said Durand, much disturbed, "we can talk it over, there. Of course, Monsieur Darrel, I have never had the faintest idea that you were the murderer!"

The four gendarmes and I walked across the road to the Groix Inn and entered the café. It was crowded with Britons, smoking, drinking, and jabbering in half a dozen dialects, all equally unsatisfactory to a civilized ear; and I pushed through the crowd to where little Max Fortin, the chemist of Quimperlé, stood smoking a vile cigar.

"This is a bad business," he said, shaking hands and offering me the mate to his cigar, which I politely declined.

" Now, Monsieur Fortin," I said, " it appears that the Purple Emperor found my handkerchief near the murdered man's door this morning, and so he concludes "—here I glared at the Purple Emperor—" that I am the assassin. I will now ask him a question," and turning on him suddenly, I shouted, " What were you doing at the Red Admiral's door? "

The Purple Emperor started and turned pale, and I pointed at him triumphantly.

" See what a sudden question will do. Look how embarrassed he is, and yet I do not charge him with murder; and I tell you, gentlemen, that man there knows as well as I do who was the murderer of the Red Admiral! "

" I don't! " bawled the Purple Emperor.

" You do," I said. " It was Yves Terrec."

" I don't believe it," he said obstinately, dropping his voice.

" Of course not, being pig-headed."

" I am not pig-headed," he roared again, " but I am mayor of St. Gildas, and I do not believe that Yves Terrec killed his father."

" You saw him try to kill him last night? "

The mayor grunted.

" And you saw what I did."

He grunted again.

" And," I went on, " you heard Yves Terrec threaten to kill his father. You heard him curse the Red Admiral and swear to kill him.

Now the father is murdered and his body is gone."

"And your handkerchief?" sneered the Purple Emperor.

"I dropped it, of course."

"And the seaweed gatherer who saw you last night lurking about the Red Admiral's cottage," grinned the Purple Emperor.

I was startled at the man's malice.

"That will do," I said. "It is perfectly true that I was walking on the Bannalec road last night, and that I stopped to close the Red Admiral's door, which was ajar, although his light was not burning. After that I went up the road to the Dinez Woods, and then walked over by St. Julien, whence I saw the seaweed gatherer on the cliffs. He was near enough for me to hear what he sang. What of that?"

"What did you do then?"

"Then I stopped at the shrine and said a prayer, and then I went to bed and slept until Brigadier Durand's gendarmes awoke me with their clatter."

"Now, Monsieur Darrel," said the Purple Emperor, lifting a fat finger and shooting a wicked glance at me, "Now, Monsieur Darrel, which did you wear last night on your midnight stroll—sabots or shoes?"

I thought a moment. "Shoes—no, sabots. I just slipped on my chaussons and went out in my sabots."

" Which was it, shoes or sabots? " snarled
the Purple Emperor.

" Sabots, you fool."

" Are these your sabots? " he asked, lifting
up a wooden shoe with my initials cut on the
instep.

" Yes," I replied.

" Then how did this blood come on the other
one? " he shouted, and held up a sabot, the mate
to the first, on which a drop of blood had spattered.

" I haven't the least idea," I said calmly;
but my heart was beating very fast and I was
furiously angry.

" You blockhead! " I said, controlling my
rage, " I'll make you pay for this when they
catch Yves Terrec and convict him. Brigadier Durand, do your duty if you think I am
under suspicion. Arrest me, but grant me
one favour. Put me in the Red Admiral's
cottage, and I'll see whether I can't find some
clew that you have overlooked. Of course,
I won't disturb anything until the Commissaire arrives. Bah! You all make me
very ill."

" He's hardened," observed the Purple Emperor, wagging his head.

" What motive had I to kill the Red Admiral? " I asked them all scornfully. And they
all cried:

" None! Yves Terrec is the man! "

Passing out of the door I swung around and shook my finger at the Purple Emperor.

"Oh, I'll make you dance for this, my friend," I said; and I followed Brigadier Durand across the street to the cottage of the murdered man.

III.

They took me at my word and placed a gendarme with a bared sabre at the gateway by the hedge.

"Give me your parole," said poor Durand, "and I will let you go where you wish." But I refused, and began prowling about the cottage looking for clews. I found lots of things that some people would have considered most important, such as ashes from the Red Admiral's pipe, footprints in a dusty vegetable bin, bottles smelling of Pouldu cider, and dust—oh, lots of dust!—but I was not an expert, only a stupid, everyday amateur; so I defaced the footprints with my thick shooting boots, and I declined to examine the pipe ashes through a microscope, although the Red Admiral's microscope stood on the table close at hand.

At last I found what I had been looking for, some long wisps of straw, curiously depressed and flattened in the middle, and I was certain I had found the evidence that would settle Yves Terrec for the rest of his life. It was plain as the nose on your face. The straws were sabot straws, flattened where the foot had pressed them, and sticking straight out where they projected beyond the sabot. Now nobody in St. Gildas used straw in sabots except a fisherman who lived near St. Julien, and the straw in his sabots was ordinary yellow wheat straw! This straw, or rather these straws, were from the stalks of the red wheat which only grows inland, and which, everybody in St. Gildas knew, Yves Terrec wore in his sabots. I was perfectly satisfied; and when, three hours later, a hoarse shouting from the Bannalec Road brought me to the window, I was not surprised to see Yves Terrec, bloody, dishevelled, hatless, with his strong arms bound behind him, walking with bent head between two mounted gendarmes. The crowd around him swelled every minute, crying: Parricide! parricide! Death to the murderer!" As he passed my window I saw great clots of mud on his dusty sabots, from the heels of which projected wisps of red wheat straw. Then I walked back into the Red Admiral's study, determined to find what the microscope would show on the wheat straws. I examined each one very carefully, and then, my eyes aching, I rested my chin on my hand and leaned back in the chair. I had not been as fortunate as some detectives, for there was no evidence that the straws had ever been used in a sabot at all. Furthermore, directly across the hallway stood a carved Breton chest, and now I noticed for the first time that, from beneath the closed lid, doxens of similar red wheat straws projected, bent exactly as mine were bent by the weight of the lid.

I yawned in disgust. It was apparent that I was not cut out for a detective, and I bitterly pondered over the difference between clews in real life and clews in a detective story. After a while I rose, walked over to the chest and opened the lid. The interior was wadded with the red wheat straws, and on this wadding lay two curious glass jars, two or three small vials, several empty bottles labelled chloroform, a collecting jar of cyanide of potassium, and a book. In a farther corner of the chest were some letters bearing English stamps, and also the torn coverings of two parcels, all from England, and all directed to the Red Admiral under his proper name of " Sieur Louis Jean Terrec, St. Gildas, par Moëlan, Finistère."

All these traps I carried over to the desk, shut the lid of the chest, and sat down to read the letters. They were written in commercial French, evidently by an Englishman.

Freely translated, the contents of the first letter were as follows:

"LONDON, *June 12, 1894.*

" DEAR MONSIEUR (*sic*): Your kind favour of the 19th inst. received and contents noted. The latest work on the Lepidoptera of England is Blowzer's How to catch British

Butterflies, with notes and tables, and an introduction by Sir Thomas Sniffer. The price of this work (in one volume, calf) is £5 or 125 francs of French money. A post-office order will receive our prompt attention. We beg to remain,

"Yours, etc.,
"FRADLEY & TOOMER,
"470 Regent Square, London, S. W."

The next letter was even less interesting. It merely stated that the money had been received and the book would be forwarded. The third engaged my attention, and I shall quote it, the translation being a free one:

"DEAR SIR: Your letter of the 1st of July was duly received, and we at once referred it to Mr. Fradley himself. Mr. Fradley being much interested in your question, sent your letter to Professor Schweineri, of the Berlin Entomological Society, whose note Blowzer refers to on page 630, in his How to catch British Butterflies. We have just received an answer from Professor Schweineri, which we translate into French—(see inclosed slip). Professor Schweineri begs to present to you two jars of cythyl, prepared under his own supervision. We forward the same to you. Trusting that you will find everything satisfactory, we remain,

"Yours sincerely,
"FRADLEY & TOOMER."

The inclosed slip read as follows:

"Messrs. FRADLEY & TOOMER,

"GENTLEMEN: Cythaline, a complex hydrocarbon, was first used by Professor Schnoot, of Antwerp, a year ago. I discovered an analogous formula about the same time and named it cythyl. I have used it with great success everywhere. It is as certain as a magnet. I beg to present you three small jars, and would be pleased to have you forward two of them to your correspondent in St. Gildas with my compliments. Blowzer's quotation of me, on page 630 of his glorious work, How to catch British Butterflies, is correct.

"Yours, etc.,

"HEINRICH SCHWEINERI,

P. H. D., D. D., D. S., M. S."

When I had finished this letter I folded it up and put it into my pocket with the others. Then I opened Blowzer's valuable work, How to catch British Butterflies, and turned to page 630.

Now, although the Red Admiral could only have acquired the book very recently, and although all the other pages were perfectly clean, this particular page was thumbed black, and heavy pencil marks inclosed a paragraph at the bottom of the page. This is the paragraph:

"Professor Schweineri says: 'Of the two old methods used by collectors for the capture of the swift-winged, high-flying Apatura Iris, or Purple Emperor, the first, which was using a long-handled net, proved successful once in a thousand times; and the second, the placing of bait upon the ground, such as decayed meat, dead cats, rats, etc., was not only disagreeable, even for an enthusiastic collector, but also very uncertain. Once in five hundred times would the splendid butterfly leave the tops of his favourite oak trees to circle about the fetid bait offered. I have found cythyl a perfectly sure bait to draw this beautiful butterfly to the ground, where it can be easily captured. An ounce of cythyl placed in a yellow saucer under an oak tree, will draw to it every Apatura Iris within a radius of twenty miles. So, if any collector who possesses a little cythyl, even though it be in a sealed bottle in his pocket—if such a collector does not find a single Apatura Iris fluttering close about him within an hour, let him be satisfied that the Apatura Iris does not inhabit his country.' "

When I had finished reading this note I sat for a long while thinking hard. Then I examined the two jars. They were labelled " *Cythyl.*" One was full, the other *nearly full.* " The rest must be on the corpse of the Red Admiral," I thought, " no matter if it is in a corked bottle——"

I took all the things back to the chest, laid

them carefully on the straw, and closed the lid. The gendarme sentinel at the gate saluted me respectfully as I crossed over to the Groix Inn. The Inn was surrounded by an excited crowd, and the hallway was choked with gendarmes and peasants. On every side they greeted me cordially, announcing that the real murderer was caught; but I pushed by them without a word and ran upstairs to find Lys. She opened her door when I knocked and threw both arms about my neck. I took her to my breast and kissed her. After a moment I asked her if she would obey me no matter what I commanded, and she said she would, with a proud humility that touched me.

" Then go at once to Yvette in St. Julien," I said. " Ask her to harness the dog-cart and drive you to the convent in Quimperlé. Wait for me there. Will you do this without questioning me, my darling? "

She raised her face to mine. " Kiss me," she said innocently; the next moment she had vanished.

I walked deliberately into the Purple Emperor's room and peered into the gauze-covered box which had held the chrysalis of Apatura Iris. It was as I expected. The chrysalis was empty and transparent, and a great crack ran down the middle of its back, but, on the netting inside the box, a magnificent butterfly slowly waved its burnished purple wings; for the

chrysalis had given up its silent tenant, the butterfly symbol of immortality. Then a great
fear fell upon me. I know now that it was
the fear of the Black Priest, but neither then
nor for years after did I know that the Black
Priest had ever lived on earth. As I bent
over the box I heard a confused murmur
outside the house which ended in a furious
shout of "Parricide!" and I heard the
gendarmes ride away behind a wagon which
rattled sharply on the flinty highway. I went
to the window. In the wagon sat Yves Terrec,
bound and wild-eyed, two gendarmes at either
side of him, and all around the wagon rode
mounted gendarmes whose bared sabres scarcely kept the crowd away.

"Parricide!" they howled. "Let him
die!"

I stepped back and opened the gauze-covered box. Very gently but firmly I took the
splendid butterfly by its closed fore wings and
lifted it unharmed between my thumb and fore-
finger. Then, holding it concealed behind my
back, I went down into the café.

Of all the crowd that had filled it, shouting
for the death of Yves Terrec, only three persons
remained seated in front of the huge empty
fireplace. They were the Brigadier Durand,
Max Fortin, the chemist of Quimperlé, and
the Purple Emperor. The latter looked
abashed when I entered, but I paid no at-

tention to him and walked straight to the chemist.

"Monsieur Fortin," I said, "do you know much about hydrocarbons?"

"They are my specialty," he said astonished.

"Have you ever heard of such a thing as cythyl?"

"Schweineri's cythyl? Oh, yes! We use it in perfumery."

"Good!" I said. "Has it an odour?"

"No—and, yes. One is always aware of its presence, but really nobody can affirm it has an odour. It is curious," he continued, looking at me, "it is very curious you should have asked me that, for all day I have been imagining I detected the presence of cythyl."

"Do you imagine so now?" I asked.

"Yes, more than ever."

I sprang to the front door and tossed out the butterfly. The splendid creature beat the air for a moment, flitted uncertainly hither and thither, and then, to my astonishment, sailed majestically back into the café and alighted on the hearthstone. For a moment I was nonplussed, but when my eyes rested on the Purple Emperor I comprehended in a flash.

"Lift that hearthstone!" I cried to the Brigadier Durand; "pry it up with your scabbard!"

The Purple Emperor suddenly fell forward in his chair, his face ghastly white, his jaw loose with terror.

"What is cythyl?" I shouted, seizing him by the arm; but he plunged heavily from his chair, face downward on the floor, and at the same moment a cry from the chemist made me turn. There stood the Brigadier Durand, one hand supporting the hearthstone, one hand raised in horror. There stood Max Fortin, the chemist, rigid with excitement, and below, in the hollow bed where the hearthstone had rested, lay a crushed mass of bleeding human flesh, from the midst of which stared a cheap glass eye. I seized the Purple Emperor and dragged him to his feet.

"Look!" I cried; "look at your old friend, the Red Admiral!" but he only smiled in a vacant way, and rolled his head muttering; "Bait for butterflies! Cythyl! Oh, no, no, no! You can't do it, Admiral, d'ye see. I alone own the Purple Emperor! I alone am the Purple Emperor!"

And the same carriage that bore me to Quimperlé to claim my bride, carried him to Quimper, gagged and bound, a foaming, howling lunatic.

.   .   .   .

This, then, is the story of the Purple Emperor. I might tell you a pleasanter story if I chose; but concerning the fish that I had hold of, whether it was a salmon, a grilse, or a sea trout, I may not say, because I have promised Lys, and she has promised me, that no power on earth shall wring from our lips the mortifying confession that the fish escaped.

POMPE FUNÈBRE.

A wind-swept sky,
The waste of moorland stretching to the west;
The sea, low moaning in a strange unrest—
A seagull's cry.

Washed by the tide,
The rocks lie sullen in the waning light;
The foam breaks in long strips of hungry white,
Dissatisfied.

BATEMAN.

POMPE FUNÈBRE.

In the days when the keepers of the house shall tremble.

WHEN I first saw the sexton he was standing motionless behind a stone. Presently he moved on again, pausing at times, and turning right and left with that nervous, jerky motion that always chills me.

His path lay across the blighted moss and withered leaves scattered in moist layers along the bank of the little brown stream, and I, wondering what his errand might be, followed, passing silently over the rotting forest mould. Once or twice he heard me, for I saw him stop short, a blot of black and orange in the sombre woods; but he always started on again, hurrying at times as though the dead might grow impatient.

For the sexton that I followed through the November forest was one of those small creatures that God has sent to bury little things that die alone in the world. Undertaker, sexton, mute, and gravedigger in one, this thing, robed

41

in black and orange, buries all things that die unheeded by the world. And so they call it— this little beetle in black and orange—the " sexton."

How he hurried! I looked up into the gray sky where ashen branches, interlaced, swayed in unfelt winds, and I heard the dry leaves rattle in the tree tops, and the thud of acorns on the mould. A sombre bird peered at me from a heap of brush, then ran pattering over the leaves.

The sexton had reached a bit of broken ground, and was scuffling over sticks and gulleys toward a brown tuft of withered grass above. I dared not help him; besides, I could not bring myself to touch him, he was so horribly absorbed in his errand.

I halted for a moment. The eagerness of this live creature to find his dead and handle it; the odour of death and decay in this little forest world, where I had waited for spring when Lys moved among the flowering gorse, singing like a throstle in the wind—all this troubled me, and I lagged behind.

The sexton scrambled over the dead grass, raising his seared eyes at every wave of wind. The wind brought sadness with it, the scent of lifeless trees, the vague rustle of gorse buds, yellow and dry as paper flowers.

Along the stream, rotting water plants, scorched and frost-blighted, lay massed above the mud. I saw their pallid stems swaying like worms in the listless current.

The sexton had reached a mouldering stump, and now he seemed undecided. I sat down on a fallen tree, moist and bleached, that crumbled under my touch, leaving a stale odour in the air. Overhead a crow rose heavily and flapped out into the moorland; the wind rattled the stark blackthorns; a single drop of rain touched my cheek. I looked into the stream for some sign of life; there was nothing, except a shapeless creature that might have been a blindworm, lying belly upward on the mud bottom. I touched it with a stick. It was stiff and dead.

The wind among the sham paperlike gorse buds filled the woods with a silken rustle. I put out my hand and touched a yellow blossom; it felt like an immortelle on a funeral pillow.

The sexton had moved on again; something, perhaps a musty spider's web, had stuck to one leg, and he dragged it as he laboured on through the wood. Some little field mouse torn by weasel or kestrel, some crushed mole, some tiny dead pile of fur or feather, lay not far off, stricken by God or man or brother creature. And the sexton knew it—how, God knows! But he knew it, and hurried on to his tryst with the dead.

His path now lay along the edge of a tidal

inlet from the Groix River. I looked down at the gray water through the leafless branches, and I saw a small snake, head raised, swim from a submerged clot of weeds into the shadow of a rock. There was a curlew, too, somewhere in the black swamp, whose dreary, persistent call cursed the silence.

I wondered when the sexton would fly; for he could fly if he chose; it is only when the dead are near, very near, that he creeps. The soiled mess of cobweb still stuck to him, and his progress was impeded by it. Once I saw a small brown and white spider, striped like a zebra, running swiftly in his tracks, but the sexton turned and raised his two clubbed forelegs in a horrid imploring attitude that still had something of menace under it. The spider backed away and sidled under a stone.

When anything that is dying—sick and close to death—falls upon the face of the earth, something moves in the blue above, floating like a moat; then another, then others. These specks that grow out of the fathomless azure vault are jewelled flies. They come to wait for Death.

The sexton also arranges rendezvous with Death, but never waits; Death must arrive the first.

When the heavy clover is ablaze with painted wings, when bees hum and blunder among the white-thorn, or pass by like swift singing bullets, the sexton snaps open his black and orange wings and hums across the clover with the bees. Death in a scented garden, the tokens of the plague on a fair young breast, the gray flag of fear in the face of one who reels into the arms of Destruction, the sexton scrambling in the lap of spring, folding his sleek wings, unfolding them to ape the buzz of bees, passing over sweet clover tops to the putrid flesh that summons him—these things must be and will be to the end.

The sexton was running now—running fast, trailing the cobweb over twigs and mud. The edge of the wood was near, for I could see the winter wheat, like green scenery in a theatre, stretching for miles across the cliffs, crude as painted grass. And as I crept through the brittle forest fringe, I saw a figure lying face downward in the wheat—a girl's slender form, limp, motionless.

The sexton darted under her breast.

Then I threw myself down beside her, crying, "Lys! Lys!" And as I cried, the icy rain burst out across the moors, and the trees dashed their stark limbs together till the whole spectral forest tossed and danced, and the wind roared among the cliffs.

And through the Dance of Death Lys trembled in my arms, and sobbed and clung to me, murmuring that the Purple Emperor was dead; but the wind tore the words from her white lips, and flung them out across the sea, where the winter lightning lashed the stark heights of Groix.

Then the fear of death was stilled in my soul, and I raised her from the ground, holding her close.

And I saw the sexton, just beyond us, hurry across the ground and seek shelter under a little dead skylark, stiff-winged, muddy, lying alone in the rain.

In the storm, above us, a bird hovered singing through the rain. It passed us twice, still singing, and as it passed again we saw the shadow it cast upon the world was whiter than snow.

THE MESSENGER.

Little gray messenger,
Robed like painted Death,
Your robe is dust.
Whom do you seek
Among lilies and closed buds
    At dusk?

Among lilies and closed buds
    At dusk,
Whom do you seek,
Little gray messenger,
Robed in the awful panoply
Of painted Death?

                              R. W. C.

48

THE MESSENGER.

All-wise,
Hast thou seen all there is to see with thy two eyes?
Dost thou know all there is to know, and so,
Omniscient,
Darest thou still to say thy brother lies?

R. W. C.

"THE bullet entered here," said Max Fortin, and he placed his middle finger over a
smooth hole exactly in the centre of the forehead.

I sat down upon a mound of dry seaweed
and unslung my fowling piece.

The little chemist cautiously felt the edges
of the shot-hole, first with his middle finger,
then with his thumb.

"Let me see the skull again," said I.

Max Fortin picked it up from the sod.

"It's like all the others," he observed. I
nodded, without offering to take it from him.
After a moment he thoughtfully replaced it
upon the grass at my feet.

"It's like all the others," he repeated, wiping his glasses on his handkerchief. "I

49

thought you might care to see one of the skulls, so I brought this over from the gravel pit. The men from Bannalec are digging yet. They ought to stop."

"How many skulls are there altogether?" I inquired.

"They found thirty-eight skulls; there are thirty-nine noted in the list. They lie piled up in the gravel pit on the edge of Le Bihan's wheat field. The men are at work yet. Le Bihan is going to stop them."

"Let's go over," said I; and I picked up my gun and started across the cliffs, Fortin on one side, Môme on the other.

"Who has the list?" I asked, lighting my pipe. "You say there is a list?"

"The list was found rolled up in a brass cylinder," said the little chemist. He added: "You should not smoke here. You know that if a single spark drifted into the wheat——"

"Ah, but I have a cover to my pipe," said I, smiling.

Fortin watched me as I closed the pepper-box arrangement over the glowing bowl of the pipe. Then he continued:

"The list was made out on thick yellow paper; the brass tube has preserved it. It is as fresh to-day as it was in 1760. You shall see it."

"Is that the date?"

"The list is dated 'April, 1760.' The

Brigadier Durand has it. It is not written in French."

"Not written in French!" I exclaimed.

"No," replied Fortin solemnly, "it is written in Breton."

"But," I protested, "the Breton language was never written or printed in 1760."

"Except by priests," said the chemist.

"I have heard of but one priest who ever wrote the Breton language," I began.

Fortin stole a glance at my face.

"You mean — the Black Priest?" he asked.

I nodded.

Fortin opened his mouth to speak again, hesitated, and finally shut his teeth obstinately over the wheat stem that he was chewing.

"And the Black Priest?" I suggested encouragingly. But I knew it was useless; for it is easier to move the stars from their courses than to make an obstinate Breton talk. We walked on for a minute or two in silence.

"Where is the Brigadier Durand?" I asked, motioning Môme to come out of the wheat, which he was trampling as though it were heather. As I spoke we came in sight of the farther edge of the wheat field and the dark, wet mass of cliffs beyond.

"Durand is down there—you can see him; he stands just behind the Mayor of St. Gildas."

"I see," said I; and we struck straight

down, following a sun-baked cattle path across the heather.

When we reached the edge of the wheat field, Le Bihan, the Mayor of St. Gildas, called to me, and I tucked my gun under my arm and skirted the wheat to where he stood.

"Thirty-eight skulls," he said in his thin, high-pitched voice; "there is but one more, and I am opposed to further search. I suppose Fortin told you?"

I shook hands with him, and returned the salute of the Brigadier Durand.

"I am opposed to further search," repeated Le Bihan, nervously picking at the mass of silver buttons which covered the front of his velvet and broadcloth jacket like a breastplate of scale armour.

Durand pursed up his lips, twisted his tremendous mustache, and hooked his thumbs in his sabre belt.

"As for me," he said, "I am in favour of further search."

"Further search for what—for the thirty-ninth skull?" I asked.

Le Bihan nodded. Durand frowned at the sunlit sea, rocking like a bowl of molten gold from the cliffs to the horizon. I followed his eyes. On the dark glistening cliffs, silhouetted against the glare of the sea, sat a cormorant, black, motionless, its horrible head raised toward heaven.

"Where is that list, Durand?" I asked.

The gendarme rummaged in his despatch pouch and produced a brass cylinder about a foot long. Very gravely he unscrewed the head and dumped out a scroll of thick yellow paper closely covered with writing on both sides. At a nod from Le Bihan he handed me the scroll. But I could make nothing of the coarse writing, now faded to a dull brown.

"Come, come, Le Bihan," I said impatiently, "translate it, won't you? You and Max Fortin make a lot of mystery out of nothing, it seems."

Le Bihan went to the edge of the pit where the three Bannalec men were digging, gave an order or two in Breton, and turned to me.

As I came to the edge of the pit the Bannalec men were removing a square piece of sailcloth from what appeared to be a pile of cobblestones.

"Look!" said Le Bihan shrilly. I looked. The pile below was a heap of skulls. After a moment I clambered down the gravel sides of the pit and walked over to the men of Bannalec. They saluted me gravely, leaning on their picks and shovels, and wiping their sweating faces with sunburned hands.

"How many?" said I in Breton.

"Thirty-eight," they replied.

I glanced around. Beyond the heap of skulls lay two piles of human bones. Beside these was a mound of broken, rusted bits of iron and steel. Looking closer, I saw that this mound was composed of rusty bayonets, sabre blades, scythe blades, with here and there a tarnished buckle attached to a bit of leather hard as iron.

I picked up a couple of buttons and a belt plate. The buttons bore the royal arms of England; the belt plate was emblazoned with the English arms, and also with the number " 27."

" I have heard my grandfather speak of the terrible English regiment, the 27th Foot, which landed and stormed the fort up there," said one of the Bannalec men.

" Oh! " said I; " then these are the bones of English soldiers? "

" Yes," said the men of Bannalec.

Le Bihan was calling to me from the edge of the pit above, and I handed the belt plate and buttons to the men and climbed the side of the excavation.

" Well," said I, trying to prevent Môme from leaping up and licking my face as I emerged from the pit, " I suppose you know what these bones are. What are you going to do with them? "

" There was a man," said Le Bihan angrily, " an Englishman, who passed here in a dogcart on his way to Quimper about an hour ago, and what do you suppose he wished to do? "

"Buy the relics?" I asked, smiling.

"Exactly—the pig!" piped the mayor of St. Gildas. "Jean Marie Tregunc, who found the bones, was standing there where Max Fortin stands, and do you know what he answered? He spat upon the ground, and said: 'Pig of an Englishman, do you take me for a desecrator of graves?'"

I knew Tregunc, a sober, blue-eyed Breton, who lived from one year's end to the other without being able to afford a single bit of meat for a meal.

"How much did the Englishman offer Tregunc?" I asked.

"Two hundred francs for the skulls alone."

I thought of the relic hunters and the relic buyers on the battlefields of our civil war.

"Seventeen hundred and sixty is long ago," I said.

"Respect for the dead can never die," said Fortin.

"And the English soldiers came here to kill your fathers and burn your homes," I continued.

"They were murderers and thieves, but—they are dead," said Tregunc, coming up from the beach below, his long sea rake balanced on his dripping jersey.

"How much do you earn every year, Jean Marie?" I asked, turning to shake hands with him.

"Two hundred and twenty francs, monsieur."

"Forty-five dollars a year," I said. "Bah! you are worth more, Jean. Will you take care of my garden for me? My wife wished me to ask you. I think it would be worth one hundred francs a month to you and to me. Come on, Le Bihan—come along, Fortin—and you, Durand. I want somebody to translate that list into French for me."

Tregunc stood gazing at me, his blue eyes dilated.

"You may begin at once," I said, smiling, "if the salary suits you?"

"It suits," said Tregunc, fumbling for his pipe in a silly way that annoyed Le Bihan.

"Then go and begin your work," cried the mayor impatiently; and Tregunc started across the moors toward St. Gildas, taking off his velvet-ribboned cap to me and gripping his sea rake very hard.

"You offer him more than my salary," said the mayor, after a moment's contemplation of his silver buttons.

"Pooh!" said I, "what do you do for your salary except play dominoes with Max Fortin at the Groix Inn?"

Le Bihan turned red, but Durand rattled his sabre and winked at Max Fortin, and I slipped my arm through the arm of the sulky magistrate, laughing.

"There's a shady spot under the cliff," I said; "come on, Le Bihan, and read me what is in the scroll."

In a few moments we reached the shadow of the cliff, and I threw myself upon the turf, chin on hand, to listen.

The gendarme, Durand, also sat down, twisting his mustache into needlelike points. Fortin leaned against the cliff, polishing his glasses and examining us with vague, near-sighted eyes; and Le Bihan, the mayor, planted himself in our midst, rolling up the scroll and tucking it under his arm.

"First of all," he began in a shrill voice, "I am going to light my pipe, and while lighting it I shall tell you what I have heard about the attack on the fort yonder. My father told me; his father told him."

He jerked his head in the direction of the ruined fort, a small, square stone structure on the sea cliff, now nothing but crumbling walls. Then he slowly produced a tobacco pouch, a bit of flint and tinder, and a long-stemmed pipe fitted with a microscopical bowl of baked clay. To fill such a pipe requires ten minutes' close attention. To smoke it to a finish takes but four puffs. It is very Breton, this Breton pipe. It is the crystallization of everything Breton.

"Go on," said I, lighting a cigarette.

"The fort," said the mayor, "was built by Louis XIV, and was dismantled twice by the

English. Louis XV restored it in 1739. In 1760 it was carried by assault by the English. They came across from the island of Groix—three shiploads—and they stormed the fort and sacked St. Julien yonder, and they started to burn St. Gildas—you can see the marks of their bullets on my house yet; but the men of Bannalec and the men of Lorient fell upon them with pike and scythe and blunderbuss, and those who did not run away lie there below in the gravel pit now—thirty-eight of them."

" And the thirty-ninth skull? " I asked, finishing my cigarette.

The mayor had succeeded in filling his pipe, and now he began to put his tobacco pouch away.

" The thirty-ninth skull," he mumbled, holding the pipestem between his defective teeth—" the thirty-ninth skull is no business of mine. I have told the Bannalec men to cease digging."

" But what is—whose is the missing skull? " I persisted curiously.

The mayor was busy trying to strike a spark to his tinder. Presently he set it aglow, applied it to his pipe, took the prescribed four puffs, knocked the ashes out of the bowl, and gravely replaced the pipe in his pocket.

" The missing skull? " he asked.

" Yes," said I impatiently.

The mayor slowly unrolled the scroll and

began to read, translating from the Breton into French. And this is what he read:

"ON THE CLIFFS OF ST. GILDAS,
"*April 13, 1760.*

"On this day, by order of the Count of Soisic, general in chief of the Breton forces now lying in Kerselec Forest, the bodies of thirty-eight English soldiers of the 27th, 50th, and 72d regiments of Foot were buried in this spot, together with their arms and equipments."

The mayor paused and glanced at me reflectively.

"Go on, Le Bihan," I said.

"With them," continued the mayor, turning the scroll and reading on the other side, "was buried the body of that vile traitor who betrayed the fort to the English. The manner of his death was as follows: By order of the most noble Count of Soisic, the traitor was first branded upon the forehead with the brand of an arrowhead. The iron burned through the flesh, and was pressed heavily so that the brand should even burn into the bone of the skull. The traitor was then led out and bidden to kneel. He admitted having guided the English from the island of Groix. Although a priest and a Frenchman, he had violated his priestly office to aid him in discovering the password to the fort. This password he extorted during confession from a young Breton girl who was in the habit of rowing across from the island of Groix to visit her husband in the fort. When the fort fell, this young girl, crazed by the death of her husband, sought the Count of Soisic and told how the priest had forced her to confess to him all she knew about the fort. The priest was arrested at St. Gildas as he was about to cross the river to Lorient. When arrested he cursed the girl, Marie Trevec——"

"What!" I exclaimed, "Marie Trevec!"

"Marie Trevec," repeated Le Bihan; "the priest cursed Marie Trevec, and all her family and descendants. He was shot as he knelt, having a mask of leather over his face, because the Bretons who composed the squad of execution refused to fire at a priest unless his face was concealed. The priest was l'Abbé Sorgue, commonly known as the Black Priest on account of his dark face and swarthy eyebrows. He was buried with a stake through his heart."

Le Bihan paused, hesitated, looked at me, and handed the manuscript back to Durand. The gendarme took it and slipped it into the brass cylinder.

"So," said I, "the thirty-ninth skull is the skull of the Black Priest."

"Yes," said Fortin. "I hope they won't find it."

"I have forbidden them to proceed," said

the mayor querulously. "You heard me, Max Fortin."

I rose and picked up my gun. Môme came and pushed his head into my hand.

"That's a fine dog," observed Durand, also rising.

"Why don't you wish to find his skull?" I asked Le Bihan. "It would be curious to see whether the arrow brand really burned into the bone."

"There is something in that scroll that I didn't read to you," said the mayor grimly. "Do you wish to know what it is?"

"Of course," I replied in surprise.

"Give me the scroll again, Durand," he said; then he read from the bottom: "I, l'Abbé Sorgue, forced to write the above by my executioners, have written it in my own blood; and with it I leave my curse. My curse on St. Gildas, on Marie Trevec, and on her descendants. I will come back to St. Gildas when my remains are disturbed. Woe to that Englishman whom my branded skull shall touch!"

"What rot!" I said. "Do you believe it was really written in his own blood?"

"I am going to test it," said Fortin, "at the request of Monsieur le Maire. I am not anxious for the job, however."

"See," said Le Bihan, holding out the scroll to me, "it is signed, 'l'Abbé Sorgue.'"

I glanced curiously over the paper.

"It must be the Black Priest," I said. "He was the only man who wrote in the Breton language. This is a wonderfully interesting discovery, for now, at last, the mystery of the Black Priest's disappearance is cleared up. You will, of course, send this scroll to Paris, Le Bihan?"

"No," said the mayor obstinately, "it shall be buried in the pit below where the rest of the Black Priest lies."

I looked at him and recognised that argument would be useless. But still I said, "It will be a loss to history, Monsieur Le Bihan."

"All the worse for history, then," said the enlightened Mayor of St. Gildas.

We had sauntered back to the gravel pit while speaking. The men of Bannalec were carrying the bones of the English soldiers toward the St. Gildas cemetery, on the cliffs to the east, where already a knot of white-coiffed women stood in attitudes of prayer; and I saw the sombre robe of a priest among the crosses of the little graveyard.

"They were thieves and assassins; they are dead now," muttered Max Fortin.

"Respect the dead," repeated the Mayor of St. Gildas, looking after the Bannalec men.

"It was written in that scroll that Marie Trevec, of Groix Island, was cursed by the priest—she and her descendants," I said, touching Le Bihan on the arm. "There was a Marie

Trevec who married an Yves Trevec of St. Gildas——"

"It is the same," said Le Bihan, looking at me obliquely.

"Oh!" said I; "then they were ancestors of my wife."

"Do you fear the curse?" asked Le Bihan.

"What?" I laughed.

"There was the case of the Purple Emperor," said Max Fortin timidly.

Startled for a moment, I faced him, then shrugged my shoulders and kicked at a smooth bit of rock which lay near the edge of the pit, almost embedded in gravel.

"Do you suppose the Purple Emperor drank himself crazy because he was descended from Marie Trevec?" I asked contemptuously.

"Of course not," said Max Fortin hastily.

"Of course not," piped the mayor. "I only—— Hello! what's that you're kicking?"

"What?" said I, glancing down, at the same time involuntarily giving another kick. The smooth bit of rock dislodged itself and rolled out of the loosened gravel at my feet.

"The thirty-ninth skull!" I exclaimed. "By jingo, its the noddle of the Black Priest! See! there is the arrowhead branded on the front!"

The mayor stepped back. Max Fortin also retreated. There was a pause, during which I looked at them, and they looked anywhere but at me.

"I don't like it," said the mayor at last, in a husky, high voice. "I don't like it! The scroll says he will come back to St. Gildas when his remains are disturbed. I—I don't like it, Monsieur Darrel——"

"Bosh!" said I; "the poor wicked devil is where he can't get out. For Heaven's sake, Le Bihan, what is this stuff you are talking in the year of grace 1896?"

The mayor gave me a look.

"And he says 'Englishman.' You are an Englishman, Monsieur Darrel," he announced.

"You know better. You know I'm an American."

"It's all the same," said the Mayor of St. Gildas, obstinately.

"No, it isn't!" I answered, much exasperated, and deliberately pushed the skull till it rolled into the bottom of the gravel pit below.

"Cover it up," said I; "bury the scroll with it too, if you insist, but I think you ought to send it to Paris. Don't look so gloomy, Fortin, unless you believe in were-wolves and ghosts. Hey! what the—what the devil's the matter with you, anyway? What are you staring at, Le Bihan?"

"Come, come," muttered the mayor in a low, tremulous voice, "it's time we got out of this. Did you see? Did you see, Fortin?"

"I saw," whispered Max Fortin, pallid with fright.

The two men were almost running across the sunny pasture now, and I hastened after them, demanding to know what was the matter.

"Matter!" chattered the mayor, gasping with exasperation and terror. "The skull is rolling uphill again!" and he burst into a terrified gallop. Max Fortin followed close behind.

I watched them stampeding across the pasture, then turned toward the gravel pit, mystified, incredulous. The skull was lying on the edge of the pit, exactly where it had been before I pushed it over the edge. For a second I stared at it; a singular chilly feeling crept up my spinal column, and I turned and walked away, sweat starting from the root of every hair on my head. Before I had gone twenty paces the absurdity of the whole thing struck me. I halted, hot with shame and annoyance, and retraced my steps.

There lay the skull.

"I rolled a stone down instead of the skull," I muttered to myself. Then with the butt of my gun I pushed the skull over the edge of the pit and watched it roll to the bottom; and as it struck the bottom of the pit, Môme, my dog, suddenly whipped his tail between his legs, whimpered, and made off across the moor.

" Môme! " I shouted, angry and astonished; but the dog only fled the faster, and I ceased calling from sheer surprise.

" What the mischief is the matter with that dog! " I thought. He had never before played me such a trick.

Mechanically I glanced into the pit, but I could not see the skull. I looked down. The skull lay at my feet again, touching them.

" Good heavens! " I stammered, and struck at it blindly with my gunstock. The ghastly thing flew into the air, whirling over and over, and rolled again down the sides of the pit to the bottom. Breathlessly I stared at it, then, confused and scarcely comprehending, I stepped back from the pit, still facing it, one, ten, twenty paces, my eyes almost starting from my head, as though I expected to see the thing roll up from the bottom of the pit under my very gaze. At last I turned my back to the pit and strode out across the gorse-covered moorland toward my home. As I reached the road that winds from St. Gildas to St. Julien I gave one hasty glance at the pit over my shoulder. The sun shone hot on the sod about the excavation. There was something white and bare and round on the turf at the edge of the pit. It might have been a stone; there were plenty of them lying about.

II.

When I entered my garden I saw Môme sprawling on the stone doorstep. He eyed me sideways and flopped his tail.

"Are you not mortified, you idiot dog?" I said, looking about the upper windows for Lys.

Môme rolled over on his back and raised one deprecating forepaw, as though to ward off calamity.

"Don't act as though I was in the habit of beating you to death," I said, disgusted. I had never in my life raised whip to the brute. "But you are a fool dog," I continued. "No, you needn't come to be babied and wept over; Lys can do that, if she insists, but I am ashamed of you, and you can go to the devil."

Môme slunk off into the house, and I followed, mounting directly to my wife's boudoir. It was empty.

"Where has she gone?" I said, looking hard at Môme, who had followed me. "Oh! I see you don't know. Don't pretend you do. Come off that lounge! Do you think Lys wants tan-coloured hairs all over her lounge?"

I rang the bell for Catherine and 'Fine, but they didn't know where "madame" had gone; so I went into my room, bathed, exchanged my somewhat grimy shooting clothes for a suit of warm, soft knickerbockers, and, after lingering some extra moments over my toilet—for I was particular, now that I had married Lys—I went down to the garden and took a chair out under the fig-trees.

"Where can she be?" I wondered. Môme came sneaking out to be comforted, and I forgave him for Lys's sake, whereupon he frisked.

"You bounding cur," said I, "now what on earth started you off across the moor? If you do it again I'll push you along with a charge of dust shot."

As yet I had scarcely dared think about the ghastly hallucination of which I had been a victim, but now I faced it squarely, flushing a little with mortification at the thought of my hasty retreat from the gravel pit.

"To think," I said aloud, "that those old woman's tales of Max Fortin and Le Bihan should have actually made me see what didn't exist at all! I lost my nerve like a schoolboy in a dark bedroom." For I knew now that I had mistaken a round stone for a skull each time, and had pushed a couple of big pebbles into the pit instead of the skull itself.

"By jingo!" said I, "I'm nervous; my liver must be in a devil of a condition if I see such things when I'm awake! Lys will know what to give me."

I felt mortified and irritated and sulky, and thought disgustedly of Le Bihan and Max Fortin.

But after a while I ceased speculating, dismissed the mayor, the chemist, and the skull from my mind, and smoked pensively, watching the sun low dipping in the western ocean. As the twilight fell for a moment over ocean and moorland, a wistful, restless happiness filled my heart, the happiness that all men know—all men who have loved.

Slowly the purple mist crept out over the sea; the cliffs darkened; the forest was shrouded.

Suddenly the sky above burned with the afterglow, and the world was alight again.

Cloud after cloud caught the rose dye; the cliffs were tinted with it; moor and pasture, heather and forest burned and pulsated with the gentle flush. I saw the gulls turning and tossing above the sand bar, their snowy wings tipped with pink; I saw the sea swallows sheering the surface of the still river, stained to its placid depths with warm reflections of the clouds. The twitter of drowsy hedge birds broke out in the stillness; a salmon rolled its shining side above tide-water.

The interminable monotone of the ocean intensified the silence. I sat motionless, holding my breath as one who listens to the first low rumour of an organ. All at once the pure whistle of a nightingale cut the silence, and the first moonbeam silvered the wastes of mist-hung waters.

I raised my head.

Lys stood before me in the garden.

When we had kissed each other, we linked arms and moved up and down the gravel walks, watching the moonbeams sparkle on the sand bar as the tide ebbed and ebbed. The broad beds of white pinks about us were atremble with hovering white moths; the October roses hung all abloom, perfuming the salt wind.

"Sweetheart," I said, "where is Yvonne? Has she promised to spend Christmas with us?"

"Yes, Dick; she drove me down from Plougat this afternoon. She sent her love to you. I am not jealous. What did you shoot?"

"A hare and four partridges. They are in the gun room. I told Catherine not to touch them until you had seen them."

Now I suppose I knew that Lys could not be particularly enthusiastic over game or guns; but she pretended she was, and always scornfully denied that it was for my sake and not for the pure love of sport. So she dragged me off to inspect the rather meagre game bag, and she paid me pretty compliments and gave a little cry of delight and pity as I lifted the enormous hare out of the sack by his ears.

"He'll eat no more of our lettuce," I said, attempting to justify the assassination.

"Unhappy little bunny—and what a beauty! O Dick, you are a splendid shot, are you not?"

I evaded the question and hauled out a partridge.

"Poor little dead things!" said Lys in a whisper; "it seems a pity—doesn't it, Dick? But then you are so clever——"

"We'll have them broiled," I said guardedly; "tell Catherine."

Catherine came in to take away the game, and presently 'Fine Lelocard, Lys's maid, announced dinner, and Lys tripped away to her boudoir.

I stood an instant contemplating her blissfully, thinking, "My boy, you're the happiest fellow in the world—you're in love with your wife!"

I walked into the dining room, beamed at the plates, walked out again; met Tregunc in the hallway, beamed on him; glanced into the kitchen, beamed at Catherine, and went up stairs, still beaming.

Before I could knock at Lys's door it opened, and Lys came hastily out. When she saw me she gave a little cry of relief, and nestled close to my breast.

"There is something peering in at my window," she said.

"What!" I cried angrily.

"A man, I think, disguised as a priest, and he has a mask on. He must have climbed up by the bay tree."

I was down the stairs and out of doors in no time. The moonlit garden was absolutely deserted. Tregunc came up, and together we searched the hedge and shrubbery around the house and out to the road.

"Jean Marie," said I at length, "loose my bulldog—he knows you—and take your supper on the porch where you can watch. My wife says the fellow is disguised as a priest, and wears a mask."

Tregunc showed his white teeth in a smile. "He will not care to venture in here again, I think, Monsieur Darrel."

I went back and found Lys seated quietly at the table.

"The soup is ready, dear," she said. "Don't worry; it was only some foolish lout from Bannalec. No one in St. Gildas or St. Julien would do such a thing."

I was too much exasperated to reply at first, but Lys treated it as a stupid joke, and after a while I began to look at it in that light.

Lys told me about Yvonne, and reminded me of my promise to have Herbert Stuart down to meet her.

"You wicked diplomat!" I protested. "Herbert is in Paris, and hard at work for the Salon."

"Don't you think he might spare a week to flirt with the prettiest girl in Finistère?" inquired Lys innocently.

"Prettiest girl! Not much!" I said.

"Who is, then?" urged Lys.

I laughed a trifle sheepishly.

"I suppose you mean me, Dick," said Lys, colouring up.

"Now I bore you, don't I?"

"Bore me? Ah, no, Dick."

After coffee and cigarettes were served I spoke about Tregunc, and Lys approved.

"Poor Jean! he will be glad, won't he? What a dear fellow you are!"

"Nonsense," said I; "we need a gardener; you said so yourself, Lys."

But Lys leaned over and kissed me, and then bent down and hugged Môme, who whistled through his nose in sentimental appreciation.

"I am a very happy woman," said Lys.

"Môme was a very bad dog to-day," I observed.

"Poor Môme!" said Lys, smiling.

When dinner was over and Môme lay snoring before the blaze—for the October nights are often chilly in Finistère—Lys curled up in the chimney corner with her embroidery, and gave me a swift glance from under her drooping lashes.

"You look like a schoolgirl, Lys," I said teasingly. "I don't believe you are sixteen yet."

She pushed back her heavy burnished hair thoughtfully. Her wrist was as white as surf foam.

"Have we been married four years? I don't believe it," I said.

She gave me another swift glance and touched the embroidery on her knee, smiling faintly.

"I see," said I, also smiling at the embroidered garment. "Do you think it will fit?"

"Fit?" repeated Lys. Then she laughed.

"And," I persisted, "are you perfectly sure that you—er—we shall need it?"

"Perfectly," said Lys. A delicate colour touched her cheeks and neck. She held up the little garment, all fluffy with misty lace and wrought with quaint embroidery.

"It is very gorgeous," said I; "don't use your eyes too much, dearest. May I smoke a pipe?"

"Of course," she said, selecting a skein of pale blue silk.

For a while I sat and smoked in silence, watching her slender fingers among the tinted silks and thread of gold.

Presently she spoke: "What did you say your crest is, Dick?"

"My crest? Oh, something or other rampant on a something or other——"

"Dick!"

"Dearest?"

"Don't be flippant."

"But I really forget. It's an ordinary crest; everybody in New York has them. No family should be without 'em."

"You are disagreeable, Dick. Send Josephine upstairs for my album."

"Are you going to put that crest on the—the—whatever it is?"

"I am; and my own crest, too."

I thought of the Purple Emperor and wondered a little.

"You didn't know I had one, did you?" she smiled.

"What is it?" I replied evasively.

"You shall see. Ring for Josephine."

I rang, and, when 'Fine appeared, Lys gave her some orders in a low voice, and Josephine trotted away, bobbing her white-coiffed head with a "Bien, madame!"

After a few minutes she returned, bearing a tattered, musty volume, from which the gold and blue had mostly disappeared.

I took the book in my hands and examined the ancient emblazoned covers.

"Lilies!" I exclaimed.

"Fleur-de-lis," said my wife demurely.

"Oh!" said I, astonished, and opened the book.

"You have never before seen this book?" asked Lys, with a touch of malice in her eyes.

"You know I haven't. Hello! what's this? Oho! So there should be a *de* before Trevec? Lys de Trevec? Then why in the world did the Purple Emperor——"

"Dick!" cried Lys.

"All right," said I. "Shall I read about the Sieur de Trevec who rode to Saladin's tent alone to seek for medicine for St. Louis? or shall I read about—what is it? Oh, here it is, all down in black and white—about the Marquis de Trevec who drowned himself before Alva's eyes rather than surrender the banner of the fleur-de-lis to Spain? It's all written here. But, dear, how about that soldier named Trevec who was killed in the old fort on the cliff yonder?"

"He dropped the *de*, and the Trevecs since then have been Republicans," said Lys—"all except me."

"That's quite right," said I; "it is time that we Republicans should agree upon some feudal system. My dear, I drink to the king!" and I raised my wine-glass and looked at Lys.

"To the king," said Lys, flushing. She smoothed out the tiny garment on her knees; she touched the glass with her lips; her eyes were very sweet. I drained the glass to the king.

After a silence I said: "I will tell the king stories. His Majesty shall be amused."

"His Majesty," repeated Lys softly.

"Or hers," I laughed. "Who knows?"

"Who knows?" murmured Lys, with a gentle sigh.

"I know some stories about Jack the Giant-Killer," I announced. "Do you, Lys?"

"I? No, not about a giant-killer, but I know all about the were-wolf, and Jeanne-la-Flamme, and the Man in Purple Tatters, and— O dear me! I know lots more."

"You are very wise," said I. "I shall teach his Majesty English."

"And I Breton," cried Lys jealously.

"I shall bring playthings to the king," said I—"big green lizards from the gorse, little gray mullets to swim in glass globes, baby rabbits from the forest of Kerselec——"

"And I," said Lys, "will bring the first primrose, the first branch of aubepine, the first jonquil, to the king—my king."

"Our king," said I; and there was peace in Finistère.

I lay back, idly turning the leaves of the curious old volume.

"I am looking," said I, "for the crest."

"The crest, dear? It is a priest's head with an arrow-shaped mark on the forehead, on a field——"

I sat up and stared at my wife.

"Dick, whatever is the matter?" she smiled. "The story is there in that book. Do you care to read it? No? Shall I tell it to you? Well, then: It happened in the third crusade. There was a monk whom men called the Black Priest. He turned apostate, and sold himself to the enemies of Christ. A Sieur de Trevec burst into the Saracen camp, at the head of only one hundred lances, and carried the Black Priest away out of the very midst of their army."

"So that is how you come by the crest," I said quietly; but I thought of the branded skull in the gravel pit, and wondered.

"Yes," said Lys. "The Sieur de Trevec cut the Black Priest's head off, but first he branded him with an arrow mark on the forehead. The book says it was a pious action, and the Sieur de Trevec got great merit by it. But I think it was cruel, the branding," she sighed.

"Did you ever hear of any other Black Priest?"

"Yes. There was one in the last century, here in St. Gildas. He cast a white shadow in the sun. He wrote in the Breton language. Chronicles, too, I believe. I never saw them. His name was the same as that of the old chronicler, and of the other priest, Jacques Sorgue. Some said he was a lineal descendant of the traitor. Of course the first Black Priest was bad enough for anything. But if he did have a child, it need not have been the ancestor of the last Jacques Sorgue. They say this one was a holy man. They say he was so good he was not allowed to die, but was caught up to heaven one day," added Lys, with believing eyes.

I smiled.

"But he disappeared," persisted Lys.

"I'm afraid his journey was in another direction," I said jestingly, and thoughtlessly told her the story of the morning. I had utterly forgotten the masked man at her window, but before I finished I remembered him fast enough, and realized what I had done as I saw her face whiten.

"Lys," I urged tenderly, "that was only some clumsy clown's trick. You said so yourself. You are not superstitious, my dear?"

Her eyes were on mine. She slowly drew the little gold cross from her bosom and kissed it. But her lips trembled as they pressed the symbol of faith.

III.

About nine o'clock the next morning I walked into the Groix Inn and sat down at the long discoloured oaken table, nodding good-day to Marianne Bruyère, who in turn bobbed her white coiffe at me.

"My clever Bannalec maid," said I, "what is good for a stirrup-cup at the Groix Inn?"

"Schist?" she inquired in Breton.

"With a dash of red wine, then," I replied.

She brought the delicious Quimperlé cider, and I poured a little Bordeaux into it. Marianne watched me with laughing black eyes.

"What makes your cheeks so red, Marianne?" I asked. "Has Jean Marie been here?"

"We are to be married, Monsieur Darrel," she laughed.

"Ah! Since when has Jean Marie Tregunc lost his head?"

"His head? Oh, Monsieur Darrel—his heart, you mean!"

"So I do," said I. "Jean Marie is a practical fellow."

"It is all due to your kindness——" began the girl, but I raised my hand and held up the glass.

"It's due to himself. To your happiness, Marianne;" and I took a hearty draught of the schist. "Now," said I, "tell me where I can find Le Bihan and Max Fortin."

"Monsieur Le Bihan and Monsieur Fortin are above in the broad room. I believe they are examining the Red Admiral's effects."

"To send them to Paris? Oh, I know. May I go up, Marianne?"

"And God go with you," smiled the girl.

When I knocked at the door of the broad room above little Max Fortin opened it. Dust covered his spectacles and nose; his hat, with the tiny velvet ribbons fluttering, was all awry.

"Come in, Monsieur Darrel," he said; "the mayor and I are packing up the effects of the Purple Emperor and of the poor Red Admiral."

"The collections?" I asked, entering the room. "You must be very careful in packing those butterfly cases; the slightest jar might break wings and antennæ, you know."

Le Bihan shook hands with me and pointed to the great pile of boxes.

" They're all cork lined," he said, " but Fortin and I are putting felt around each box. The Entomological Society of Paris pays the freight."

The combined collections of the Red Admiral and the Purple Emperor made a magnificent display.

I lifted and inspected case after case set with gorgeous butterflies and moths, each specimen carefully labelled with the name in Latin. There were cases filled with crimson tiger moths all aflame with colour; cases devoted to the common yellow butterflies; symphonies in orange and pale yellow; cases of soft gray and dun-coloured sphinx moths; and cases of garish nettle-bred butterflies of the numerous family of *Vanessa*.

All alone in a great case by itself was pinned the purple emperor, the Apatura Iris, that fatal specimen that had given the Purple Emperor his name and quietus.

I remembered the butterfly, and stood looking at it with bent eyebrows.

Le Bihan glanced up from the floor where he was nailing down the lid of a box full of cases.

"It is settled, then," said he, " that madame,

your wife, gives the Purple Emperor's entire
collection to the city of Paris? "

I nodded.

" Without accepting anything for it? "

" It is a gift," I said.

" Including the purple emperor there in
the case? That butterfly is worth a great deal
of money," persisted Le Bihan.

" You don't suppose that we would wish to
sell that specimen, do you? " I answered a
trifle sharply.

" If I were you I should destroy it," said the
mayor in his high-pitched voice.

" That would be nonsense," said I—" like
your burying the brass cylinder and scroll yesterday."

" It was not nonsense," said Le Bihan dog-
gedly, " and I should prefer not to discuss the
subject of the scroll."

I looked at Max Fortin, who immediately
avoided my eyes.

" You are a pair of superstitious old wom-
en," said I, digging my hands into my pockets;
" you swallow every nursery tale that is in-
vented."

" What of it? " said Le Bihan sulkily;
" there's more truth than lies in most of 'em."

" Oh! " I sneered, " does the Mayor of St.
Gildas and St. Julien believe in the Loup-
garou? "

" No, not in the Loup-garou."

"In what, then—Jeanne-la-Flamme?"

"That," said Le Bihan with conviction, "is history."

"The devil it is!" said I; "and perhaps, monsieur the mayor, your faith in giants is unimpaired?"

"There were giants—everybody knows it," growled Max Fortin.

"And you a chemist!" I observed scornfully.

"Listen, Monsieur Darrel," squeaked Le Bihan; "you know yourself that the Purple Emperor was a scientific man. Now suppose I should tell you that he always refused to include in his collection a Death's Messenger?"

"A what?" I exclaimed.

"You know what I mean—that moth that flies by night; some call it the Death's Head, but in St. Gildas we call it 'Death's Messenger.'"

"Oh!" said I, "you mean that big sphinx moth that is commonly known as the 'death's-head moth.' Why the mischief should the people here call it death's messenger?"

"For hundreds of years it has been known as death's messenger in St. Gildas," said Max Fortin. "Even Froissart speaks of it in his commentaries on Jacques Sorgue's Chronicles. The book is in your library."

"Sorgue? And who was Jacques Sorgue? I never read his book."

"Jacques Sorgue was the son of some un-frocked priest—I forget. It was during the crusades."

"Good Heavens!" I burst out, "I've been hearing of nothing but crusades and priests and death and sorcery ever since I kicked that skull into the gravel pit, and I am tired of it, I tell you frankly. One would think we lived in the dark ages. Do you know what year of our Lord it is, Le Bihan?"

"Eighteen hundred and ninety-six," re-plied the mayor.

"And yet you two hulking men are afraid of a death's-head moth."

"I don't care to have one fly into the win-dow," said Max Fortin; "it means evil to the house and the people in it."

"God alone knows why he marked one of his creatures with a yellow death's head on the back," observed Le Bihan piously, "but I take it that he meant it as a warning; and I propose to profit by it," he added trium-phantly.

"See here, Le Bihan," I said; "by a stretch of imagination one can make out a skull on the thorax of a certain big sphinx moth. What of it?"

"It is a bad thing to touch," said the mayor, wagging his head.

"It squeaks when handled," added Max Fortin.

"Some creatures squeak all the time," I observed, looking hard at Le Bihan.

"Pigs," added the mayor.

"Yes, and asses," I replied. "Listen, Le Bihan: do you mean to tell me that you saw that skull roll uphill yesterday?"

The mayor shut his mouth tightly and picked up his hammer.

"Don't be obstinate," I said; "I asked you a question."

"And I refuse to answer," snapped Le Bihan. "Fortin saw what I saw; let him talk about it."

I looked searchingly at the little chemist.

"I don't say that I saw it actually roll up out of the pit, all by itself," said Fortin with a shiver, "but—but then, how did it come up out of the pit, if it didn't roll up all by itself?"

"It didn't come up at all; that was a yellow cobblestone that you mistook for the skull again," I replied. "You were nervous, Max."

"A—a very curious cobblestone, Monsieur Darrel," said Fortin.

"I also was a victim to the same hallucination," I continued, "and I regret to say that I took the trouble to roll two innocent cobblestones into the gravel pit, imagining each time that it was the skull I was rolling."

"It was," observed Le Bihan with a morose shrug.

"It just shows," said I, ignoring the

mayor's remark, " how easy it is to fix up a train
of coincidences so that the result seems to sa-
vour of the supernatural.   Now, last night my
wife imagined that she saw a priest in a mask
peer in at her window——"

Fortin and Le Bihan scrambled hastily from
their knees, dropping hammer and nails.

" W-h-a-t——what's that? " demanded the
mayor.

I repeated what I had said.   Max Fortin
turned livid.

" My God! " muttered Le Bihan, " the
Black Priest is in St. Gildas! "

" D-don't you——you know the old prophecy? " stammered Fortin; " Froissart quotes it
from Jacques Sorgue:

> ' When the Black Priest rises from the dead,
>   St. Gildas folk shall shriek in bed;
>   When the Black Priest rises from his grave,
>   May the good God St. Gildas save ! ' "

" Aristide Le Bihan," I said angrily, " and
you, Max Fortin, I've got enough of this nonsense!   Some foolish lout from Bannalec has
been in St. Gildas playing tricks to frighten old
fools like you.   If you have nothing better to
talk about than nursery legends I'll wait until
you come to your senses.   Good-morning."
And I walked out, more disturbed than I cared
to acknowledge to myself.

The day had become misty and overcast.

Heavy, wet clouds hung in the east. I heard the surf thundering against the cliffs, and the gray gulls squealed as they tossed and turned high in the sky. The tide was creeping across the river sands, higher, higher, and I saw the seaweed floating on the beach, and the *lançons* springing from the foam, silvery thread-like flashes in the gloom. Curlew were flying up the river in twos and threes; the timid sea swallows skimmed across the moors toward some quiet, lonely pool, safe from the coming tempest. In every hedge field birds were gathering, huddling together, twittering restlessly.

When I reached the cliffs I sat down, resting my chin on my clenched hands. Already a vast curtain of rain, sweeping across the ocean miles away, hid the island of Groix. To the east, behind the white semaphore on the hills, black clouds crowded up over the horizon. After a little the thunder boomed, dull, distant, and slender skeins of lightning unravelled across the crest of the coming storm. Under the cliff at my feet the surf rushed foaming over the shore, and the *lançons* jumped and skipped and quivered until they seemed to be but the reflections of the meshed lightning.

I turned to the east. It was raining over Groix, it was raining at Sainte Barbe, it was raining now at the semaphore. High in the storm whirl a few gulls pitched; a nearer cloud trailed veils of rain in its wake; the sky was spattered with lightning; the thunder boomed.

As I rose to go, a cold raindrop fell upon the back of my hand, and another, and yet another on my face. I gave a last glance at the sea, where the waves were bursting into strange white shapes that seemed to fling out menacing arms toward me. Then something moved on the cliff, something black as the black rock it clutched—a filthy cormorant, craning its hideous head at the sky.

Slowly I plodded homeward across the sombre moorland, where the gorse stems glimmered with a dull metallic green, and the heather, no longer violet and purple, hung drenched and dun-coloured among the dreary rocks. The wet turf creaked under my heavy boots, the black-thorn scraped and grated against knee and elbow. Over all lay a strange light, pallid, ghastly, where the sea spray whirled across the landscape and drove into my face until it grew numb with the cold. In broad bands, rank after rank, billow on billow, the rain burst out across the endless moors, and yet there was no wind to drive it at such a pace.

Lys stood at the door as I turned into the garden, motioning me to hasten; and then for the first time I became conscious that I was soaked to the skin.

"How ever in the world did you come to stay out when such a storm threatened?" she said. "Oh, you are dripping! Go quickly and change; I have laid your warm underwear on the bed, Dick."

I kissed my wife, and went upstairs to change my dripping clothes for something more comfortable.

When I returned to the morning room there was a driftwood fire on the hearth, and Lys sat in the chimney corner embroidering.

"Catherine tells me that the fishing fleet from Lorient is out. Do you think they are in danger, dear?" asked Lys, raising her blue eyes to mine as I entered.

"There is no wind, and there will be no sea," said I, looking out of the window. Far across the moor I could see the black cliffs looming in the mist.

"How it rains!" murmured Lys; "come to the fire, Dick."

I threw myself on the fur rug, my hands in my pockets, my head on Lys's knees.

"Tell me a story," I said. "I feel like a boy of ten."

Lys raised a finger to her scarlet lips. I always waited for her to do that.

"Will you be very still, then?" she said.

"Still as death."

"Death," echoed a voice, very softly.

"Did you speak, Lys?" I asked, turning so that I could see her face.

"No; did you, Dick?"

" Who said ' death '? " I asked, startled.

" Death," echoed a voice, softly.

I sprang up and looked about. Lys rose too, her needles and embroidery falling to the floor. She seemed about to faint, leaning heavily on me, and I led her to the window and opened it a little way to give her air. As I did so the chain lightning split the zenith, the thunder crashed, and a sheet of rain swept into the room, driving with it something that fluttered—something that flapped, and squeaked, and beat upon the rug with soft, moist wings.

We bent over it together, Lys clinging to me, and we saw that it was a death's-head moth drenched with rain.

The dark day passed slowly as we sat beside the fire, hand in hand, her head against my breast, speaking of sorrow and mystery and death. For Lys believed that there were things on earth that none might understand, things that must be nameless forever and ever, until God rolls up the scroll of life and all is ended. We spoke of hope and fear and faith, and the mystery of the saints; we spoke of the beginning and the end, of the shadow of sin, of omens, and of love. The moth still lay on the floor, quivering its sombre wings in the warmth of the fire, the skull and ribs clearly etched upon its neck and body.

" If it is a messenger of death to this house," I said, " why should we fear, Lys? "

"Death should be welcome to those who love God," murmured Lys, and she drew the cross from her breast and kissed it.

"The moth might die if I threw it out into the storm," I said after a silence.

"Let it remain," sighed Lys.

Late that night my wife lay sleeping, and I sat beside her bed and read in the Chronicle of Jacques Sorgue. I shaded the candle, but Lys grew restless, and finally I took the book down into the morning room, where the ashes of the fire rustled and whitened on the hearth.

The death's-head moth lay on the rug before the fire where I had left it. At first I thought it was dead, but, when I looked closer I saw a lambent fire in its amber eyes. The straight white shadow it cast across the floor wavered as the candle flickered.

The pages of the Chronicle of Jacques Sorgue were damp and sticky; the illuminated gold and blue initials left flakes of azure and gilt where my hand brushed them.

"It is not paper at all; it is thin parchment," I said to myself; and I held the discoloured page close to the candle flame and read, translating laboriously:

"I, Jacques Sorgue, saw all these things. And I saw the Black Mass celebrated in the chapel of St. Gildas-on-the-Cliff. And it was said by the Abbé Sorgue, my kinsman: for which deadly sin the apostate priest was seized

by the most noble Marquis of Plougastel and
by him condemned to be burned with hot irons,
until his seared soul quit its body and fly to its
master the devil. But when the Black Priest
lay in the crypt of Plougastel, his master Satan
came at night and set him free, and carried him
across land and sea to Mahmoud, which is Soldan or Saladin. And I, Jacques Sorgue,
travelling afterward by sea, beheld with my own
eyes my kinsman, the Black Priest of St. Gildas, borne along in the air upon a vast black
wing, which was the wing of his master Satan.
And this was seen also by two men of the crew."

I turned the page. The wings of the moth
on the floor began to quiver. I read on and
on, my eyes blurring under the shifting candle
flame. I read of battles and of saints, and I
learned how the great Soldan made his pact
with Satan, and then I came to the Sieur de
Trevec, and read how he seized the Black
Priest in the midst of Saladin's tents and carried him away and cut off his head, first branding him on the forehead. "And before he
suffered," said the Chronicle, "he cursed the
Sieur de Trevec and his descendants, and he
said he would surely return to St. Gildas. 'For
the violence you do to me, I will do violence to
you. For the evil I suffer at your hands, I will
work evil on you and your descendants. Woe
to your children, Sieur de Trevec!'" There
was a whirr, a beating of strong wings, and my

candle flashed up as in a sudden breeze. A humming filled the room; the great moth dated hither and thither, beating, buzzing, on ceiling and wall. I flung down my book and stepped forward. Now it lay fluttering upon the window sill, and for a moment I had it under my hand, but the thing squeaked and I shrank back. Then suddenly it darted across the candle flame; the light flared and went out, and at the same moment a shadow moved in the darkness outside. I raised my eyes to the window. A masked face was peering in at me.

Quick as thought I whipped out my revolver and fired every cartridge, but the face advanced beyond the window, the glass melting away before it like mist, and through the smoke of my revolver I saw something creep swiftly into the room. Then I tried to cry out, but the thing was at my throat, and I fell backward among the ashes of the hearth.

· · · · · · ·

When my eyes unclosed I was lying on the hearth, my head among the cold ashes. Slowly I got on my knees, rose painfully, and groped my way to a chair. On the floor lay my revolver, shining in the pale light of early morning. My mind clearing by degrees, I looked, shuddering, at the window. The glass was unbroken. I stooped stiffly, picked up my revolver and opened the cylinder. Every cartridge had been fired. Mechanically I closed the cylinder and placed the revolver in my pocket. The book, the Chronicles of Jacques Sorgue, lay on the table beside me, and as I started to close it I glanced at the page. It was all splashed with rain, and the lettering had run, so that the page was merely a confused blur of gold and red and black. As I stumbled toward the door I cast a fearful glance over my shoulder. The death's-head moth crawled shivering on the rug.

IV.

The sun was about three hours high. I must have slept, for I was aroused by the sudden gallop of horses under our window. People were shouting and calling in the road. I sprang up and opened the sash. Le Bihan was there, an image of helplessness, and Max Fortin stood beside him, polishing his glasses. Some gendarmes had just arrived from Quimperlé, and I could hear them around the corner of the house, stamping, and rattling their sabres and carbines, as they led their horses into my stable.

Lys sat up, murmuring half-sleepy, half-anxious questions.

"I don't know," I answered. "I am going out to see what it means."

"It is like the day they came to arrest you," Lys said, giving me a troubled look. But I kissed her, and laughed at her until she smiled too. Then I flung on coat and cap and hurried down the stairs.

The first person I saw standing in the road was the Brigadier Durand.

"Hello!" said I, "have you come to arrest me again? What the devil is all this fuss about, anyway?"

"We were telegraphed for an hour ago," said Durand briskly, "and for a sufficient reason, I think. Look there, Monsieur Darrel!"

He pointed to the ground almost under my feet.

"Good heavens!" I cried, "where did that puddle of blood come from?"

"That's what I want to know, Monsieur Darrel. Max Fortin found it at daybreak. See, it's splashed all over the grass, too. A trail of it leads into your garden, across the flower beds to your very window, the one that opens from the morning room. There is another trail leading from this spot across the road to the cliffs, then to the gravel pit, and thence across the moor to the forest of Kerselec. We are going to mount in a minute and search the bosquets. Will you join us? Bon Dieu! but the fellow bled like an ox. Max Fortin says it's human blood, or I should not have believed it."

The little chemist of Quimperlé came up at

that moment, rubbing his glasses with a coloured handkerchief.

"Yes, it is human blood," he said, "but one thing puzzles me: the corpuscles are yellow. I never saw any human blood before with yellow corpuscles. But your English Doctor Thompson asserts that he has——"

"Well, it's human blood, anyway—isn't it?" insisted Durand, impatiently.

"Ye-es," admitted Max Fortin.

"Then it's my business to trail it," said the big gendarme, and he called his men and gave the order to mount.

"Did you hear anything last night?" asked Durand of me.

"I heard the rain. I wonder the rain did not wash away these traces."

"They must have come after the rain ceased. See this thick splash, how it lies over and weighs down the wet grass blades. Pah!"

It was a heavy, evil-looking clot, and I stepped back from it, my throat closing in disgust.

"My theory," said the brigadier, "is this: Some of those Biribi fishermen, probably the Icelanders, got an extra glass of cognac into their hides and quarrelled on the road. Some of them were slashed, and staggered to your house. But there is only one trail, and yet— and yet, how could all that blood come from only one person? Well, the wounded man, let us say, staggered first to your house and then back here, and he wandered off, drunk and dying, God knows where. That's my theory."

"A very good one," said I calmly. "And you are going to trail him?"

"Yes."

"When?"

"At once. Will you come?"

"Not now. I'll gallop over by-and-bye. You are going to the edge of the Kerselec forest?"

"Yes; you will hear us calling. Are you coming, Max Fortin? And you, Le Bihan? Good; take the dog-cart."

The big gendarme tramped around the corner to the stable and presently returned mounted on a strong gray horse; his sabre shone on his saddle; his pale yellow and white facings were spotless. The little crowd of white-coiffed women with their children fell back, as Durand touched spurs and clattered away followed by his two troopers. Soon after Le Bihan and Max Fortin also departed in the mayor's dingy dog-cart.

"Are you coming?" piped Le Bihan shrilly.

"In a quarter of an hour," I replied, and went back to the house.

When I opened the door of the morning room the death's-head moth was beating its strong wings against the window. For a second I hesitated, then walked over and opened the sash. The creature fluttered out, whirred over the flower beds a moment, then darted across the moorland toward the sea. I called the servants together and questioned them. Josephine, Catherine, Jean Marie Tregunc, not one of them had heard the slightest disturbance during the night. Then I told Jean Marie to saddle my horse, and while I was speaking Lys came down.

"Dearest," I began, going to her.

"You must tell me everything you know, Dick," she interrupted, looking me earnestly in the face.

"But there is nothing to tell—only a drunken brawl, and some one wounded."

"And you are going to ride—where, Dick?"

"Well, over to the edge of Kerselec forest. Durand and the mayor, and Max Fortin, have gone on, following a—a trail."

"What trail?"

"Some blood."

"Where did they find it?"

"Out in the road there." Lys crossed herself.

"Does it come near our house?"

"Yes."

"How near?"

"It comes up to the morning-room window," said I, giving in.

Her hand on my arm grew heavy. "I dreamed last night——"

"So did I——" but I thought of the empty cartridges in my revolver, and stopped.

"I dreamed that you were in great danger, and I could not move hand or foot to save you; but you had your revolver, and I called out to you to fire——"

"I did fire!" I cried excitedly.

"You—you fired?"

I took her in my arms. "My darling," I said, "something strange has happened—something that I can not understand as yet. But, of course, there is an explanation. Last night I thought I fired at the Black Priest."

"Ah!" gasped Lys.

"Is that what you dreamed?"

"Yes, yes, that was it! I begged you to fire——"

"And I did."

Her heart was beating against my breast. I held her close in silence.

"Dick," she said at length, "perhaps you killed the—the thing."

"If it was human I did not miss," I answered grimly. "And it was human," I went on, pulling myself together, ashamed of having so nearly gone to pieces. "Of course it was human! The whole affair is plain enough. Not a drunken brawl, as Durand thinks; it was a drunken lout's practical joke, for which he has suffered. I suppose I must have filled him pretty full of bullets, and he has crawled away to die in Kerselec forest. It's a terrible affair; I'm sorry I fired so hastily; but that idiot Le Bihan and Max Fortin have been working on my nerves till I am as hysterical as a school-girl," I ended angrily.

"You fired—but the window glass was not shattered," said Lys in a low voice.

"Well, the window was open, then. And as for the—the rest—I've got nervous indigestion, and a doctor will settle the Black Priest for me, Lys."

I glanced out of the window at Tregunc waiting with my horse at the gate.

"Dearest, I think I had better go to join Durand and the others."

"I will go too."

"Oh, no!"

"Yes, Dick."

"Don't, Lys."

"I shall suffer every moment you are away."

"The ride is too fatiguing, and we can't tell what unpleasant sight you may come upon. Lys, you don't really think there is anything supernatural in this affair?"

"Dick," she answered gently, "I am a Bre-tonne." With both arms around my neck, my wife said, "Death is the gift of God. I do not fear it when we are together. But alone—

oh, my husband, I should fear a God who could take you away from me! "

We kissed each other soberly, simply, like two children. Then Lys hurried away to change her gown, and I paced up and down the garden waiting for her.

She came, drawing on her slender gauntlets. I swung her into the saddle, gave a hasty order to Jean Marie, and mounted.

Now, to quail under thoughts of terror on a morning like this, with Lys in the saddle beside me, no matter what had happened or might happen, was impossible. Moreover, Môme came sneaking after us. I asked Tregunc to catch him, for I was afraid he might be brained by our horses' hoofs if he followed, but the wily puppy dodged and bolted after Lys, who was trotting along the high-road. "Never mind," I thought; "if he's hit he'll live, for he has no brains to lose."

Lys was waiting for me in the road beside the Shrine of Our Lady of St. Gildas when I joined her. She crossed herself, I doffed my cap, then we shook out our bridles and galloped toward the forest of Kerselec.

We said very little as we rode. I always loved to watch Lys in the saddle. Her exquisite figure and lovely face were the incarnation of youth and grace; her curling hair glistened like threaded gold.

Out of the corner of my eye I saw the

spoiled puppy Môme come bounding cheerfully alongside, oblivious of our horses' heels. Our road swung close to the cliffs. A filthy cormorant rose from the black rocks and flapped heavily across our path. Ly's horse reared, but she pulled him down, and pointed at the bird with her riding crop.

"I see," said I; "it seems to be going our way. Curious to see a cormorant in a forest, isn't it?"

"It is a bad sign," said Lys. "You know the Morbihan proverb: 'When the cormorant turns from the sea, Death laughs in the forest, and wise woodsmen build boats.'"

"I wish," said I sincerely, "that there were fewer proverbs in Brittany."

We were in sight of the forest now; across the gorse I could see the sparkle of gendarmes' trappings, and the glitter of Le Bihan's silver-buttoned jacket. The hedge was low and we took it without difficulty, and trotted across the moor to where Le Bihan and Durand stood gesticulating.

They bowed ceremoniously to Lys as we rode up.

"The trail is horrible—it is a river," said the mayor in his squeaky voice. "Monsieur Darrel, I think perhaps madame would scarcely care to come any nearer."

Lys drew bridle and looked at me.

"It is horrible!" said Durand, walking up

beside me; " it looks as though a bleeding regiment had passed this way. The trail winds and winds about there in the thickets; we lose it at times, but we always find it again. I can't understand how one man—no, nor twenty— could bleed like that! "

A halloo, answered by another, sounded from the depths of the forest.

" It's my men; they are following the trail," muttered the brigadier. " God alone knows what is at the end! "

" Shall we gallop back, Lys? " I asked.

" No; let us ride along the western edge of the woods and dismount. The sun is so hot now, and I should like to rest for a moment," she said.

" The western forest is clear of anything disagreeable," said Durand.

" Very well," I answered; " call me, Le Bihan, if you find anything."

Lys wheeled her mare, and I followed across the springy heather, Môme trotting cheerfully in the rear.

We entered the sunny woods about a quarter of a kilometre from where we left Durand. I took Lys from her horse, flung both bridles over a limb, and, giving my wife my arm, aided her to a flat mossy rock which overhung a shallow brook gurgling among the beach trees. Lys sat down and drew off her gauntlets. Môme pushed his head into her lap, received an un-

deserved caress, and came doubtfully toward
me. I was weak enough to condone his offence,
but I made him lie down at my feet, greatly
to his disgust.

I rested my head on Lys's knees, looking up
at the sky through the crossed branches of the
trees.

"I suppose I have killed him," I said. "It
shocks me terribly, Lys."

"You could not have known, dear. He
may have been a robber, and—if—not—— Did
—have you ever fired your revolver since that
day four years ago, when the Red Admiral's
son tried to kill you? But I know you have
not."

"No," said I, wondering. "It's a fact, I
have not. Why?"

"And don't you remember that I asked
you to let me load it for you the day when
Yves went off, swearing to kill you and his
father?"

"Yes, I do remember. Well?"

"Well, I—I took the cartridges first to St.
Gildas chapel and dipped them in holy water.
You must not laugh, Dick," said Lys gently,
laying her cool hands on my lips.

"Laugh, my darling!"

Overhead the October sky was pale ame-
thyst, and the sunlight burned like orange flame
through the yellow leaves of beach and oak.
Gnats and midges danced and wavered over-

head; a spider dropped from a twig halfway to the ground and hung suspended on the end of his gossamer thread.

"Are you sleepy, dear?" asked Lys, bending over me.

"I am—a little; I scarcely slept two hours last night," I answered.

"You may sleep, if you wish," said Lys, and touched my eyes caressingly.

"Is my head heavy on your knees?"

"No, Dick."

I was already in a half doze; still I heard the brook babbling under the beeches and the humming of forest flies overhead. Presently even these were stilled.

The next thing I knew I was sitting bolt upright, my ears ringing with a scream, and I saw Lys cowering beside me, covering her white face with both hands.

As I sprang to my feet she cried again and clung to my knees. I saw my dog rush growling into a thicket, then I heard him whimper, and he came backing out, whining, ears flat, tail down. I stooped and disengaged Lys's hand.

"Don't go, Dick!" she cried. "O God, it's the Black Priest!"

In a moment I had leaped across the brook and pushed my way into the thicket. It was empty. I stared about me; I scanned every tree trunk, every bush. Suddenly I saw him.

He was seated on a fallen log, his head resting in his hands, his rusty black robe gathered around him. For a moment my hair stirred under my cap; sweat started on forehead and cheek-bone; then I recovered my reason, and understood that the man was human and was probably wounded to death. Ay, to death; for there, at my feet, lay the wet trail of blood, over leaves and stones, down into the little hollow, across to the figure in black resting silently under the trees.

I saw that he could not escape even if he had the strength, for before him, almost at his very feet, lay a deep, shining swamp.

As I stepped forward my foot broke a twig. At the sound the figure started a little, then its head fell forward again. Its face was masked. Walking up to the man, I bade him tell where he was wounded. Durand and the others broke through the thicket at the same moment and hurried to my side.

" Who are you who hide a masked face in a priest's robe? " said the gendarme loudly.

There was no answer.

" See—see the stiff blood all over his robe! " muttered Le Bihan to Fortin.

" He will not speak," said I.

" He may be too badly wounded," whispered Le Bihan.

" I saw him raise his head," I said; " my wife saw him creep up here."

Durand stepped forward and touched the figure.

"Speak!" he said.

"Speak!" quavered Fortin.

Durand waited a moment, then with a sudden upward movement he stripped off the mask and threw back the man's head. We were looking into the eye sockets of a skull. Durand stood rigid; the mayor shrieked. The skeleton burst out from its rotting robes and collapsed on the ground before us. From between the staring ribs and the grinning teeth spurted a torrent of black blood, showering the shrinking grasses; then the thing shuddered, and fell over into the black ooze of the bog. Little bubbles of iridescent air appeared from the mud; the bones were slowly engulfed, and, as the last fragments sank out of sight, up from the depths and along the bank crept a creature, shiny, shivering, quivering its wings.

It was a death's-head moth.

.   .   .   .

I wish I had time to tell you how Lys outgrew superstitions—for she never knew the truth about the affair, and she never will know, since she has promised not to read this book. I wish I might tell you about the king and his coronation, and how the coronation robe fitted. I wish that I were able to write how Yvonne and Herbert Stuart rode to a boar hunt in Quimperlé, and how the hounds raced the

quarry right through the town, overturning
three gendarmes, the notary, and an old woman.
But I am becoming garrulous, and Lys is calling me to come and hear the king say that he is
sleepy. And his Highness shall not be kept
waiting.

THE KING'S CRADLE SONG.

Seal with a seal of gold
The scroll of a life unrolled;
Swathe him deep in his purple stole;
Ashes of diamonds, crystalled coal,
Drops of gold in each scented fold.

Crimson wings of the Little Death,
Stir his hair with your silken breath;
Flaming wings of sins to be,
Splendid pinions of prophecy,
Smother his eyes with hues and dyes,
While the white moon spins and the winds arise,
And the stars drip through the skies.

Wave, O wings of the Little Death!
Seal his sight and stifle his breath,
Cover his breast with the gemmed shroud pressed;
From north to north, from west to west,
Wave, O wings of the Little Death!
Till the white moon reels in the cracking skies,
And the ghosts of God arise.

THE WHITE SHADOW.

We are no other than a moving row
Of magic shadow-shapes, that come and go
   Round with this sun-illumined lantern, held
In midnight by the master of the show.

A moment's halt—a momentary taste
Of being from the well amid the waste—
   And lo! the phantom caravan has reached
The nothing it set out from.   Oh, make haste!

Ah, Love! could you and I with him conspire
To grasp this sorry scheme of things entire,
   Would not we shatter it to bits—and then
Remould it nearer to the heart's desire!
FITZGERALD.

THE WHITE SHADOW.

Listen, then, love, and with your white hand clear
Your forehead from its cloudy hair.

I.

"THREE great hulking cousins," said she, closing her gray eyes disdainfully.

We accepted the rebuke in astonished silence. Presently she opened her eyes, and seemed surprised to see us there yet.

"O," she said, "if you think I am going to stay here until you make up your minds——"

"I've made up mine," said Donald. "We will go to the links. You may come."

"I shall not," she announced. "Walter, what do you propose?"

Walter looked at his cartridge belt and then at the little breech-loader standing in a corner of the arbour.

"Oh, I know," she said, "but I won't! I won't! I won't!"

The uncles and aunts on the piazza turned to look at us; her mother arose from a steamer-chair and came across the lawn.

" Won't what, Sweetheart? " she asked, placing both hands on her daughter's shoulders.

" Mamma, Walter wants me to shoot, and Don wants me to play golf, and I—won't! "

" She doesn't know what she wants," said I.

" Don't I? " she said, flushing with displeasure.

" Her mother might suggest something," hazarded Donald. We looked at our aunt.

" Sweetheart is spoiled," said that lady decisively. " If you children don't go away at once and have a good time, I shall find employment for her."

" Algebra? " I asked maliciously.

" How dare you! " cried Sweetheart, sitting up. " Oh, isn't he mean! isn't he ignoble! —and I've done my algebra; haven't I, mamma? "

" But your French? " I began.

Donald laughed, and so did Walter. As for Sweetheart, she arose in all the dignity of sixteen years, closed her eyes with superb insolence, and, clasping her mother's waist with one round white arm, marched out of the arbour.

" We tease her too much," said Donald.

" She's growing up fast; we ought not to call her ' Sweetheart ' when she puts her hair up," added Walter.

" She's going to put it up in October, when she goes back to school," said Donald. " Jack, she will hate you if you keep reminding her of her algebra and French."

" Then I'll stop," said I, suddenly conscious what an awful thing it would be if she hated me.

Donald's two pointers came frisking across the lawn from the kennels, and Donald picked up his gun.

" Here we go again," said I. " Donny's going to the coverts after grouse, Walter's going up on the hill with his dust-shot and arsenic, and I'm going across the fields after butterflies. Why the deuce can't we all go together, just for once? "

" And take Sweetheart ? She would like it if we all went together," said Walter; " she is tired of seeing Jack net butterflies."

" Collecting birds and shooting grouse are two different things," began Donald. " You spoil my dogs by shooting your confounded owls and humming birds."

" Oh, your precious dogs! " I cried. " Shut up, Donny, and give Sweetheart a good day's tramp. It's a pity if three cousins can't pool their pleasures for once."

Donald nodded uncertainly.

" Come on," said Walter, " we'll find Sweetheart. Jack, you get your butterfly togs and come back here."

I nodded, and watched my two cousins sauntering across the lawn—big, clean-cut fellows, resembling each other enough to be brothers instead of cousins.

We all resembled each other more or less, Donald, Walter, and I. As for Sweetheart, she looked like none of us.

It was all very well for her mother to call her Sweetheart, and for her aunts to echo it in chorus, but the time was coming when we saw we should have to stop. A girl of sixteen with such a name is ridiculous, and Sweetheart was nearly seventeen; and her hair was "going up" and her gowns were "coming down" in October.

Her own name was pretty enough. I don't know that I ought to tell it, but I will: it was the same as her mother's. We called her Sweetheart sometimes, sometimes "The Aspen Beauty." Donald had given her that name from a butterfly in my collection, the Vanessa Pandora, commonly known as the Aspen beauty, from its never having been captured in America except in our village of Aspen.

Here, in the north of New York State, we four cousins spent our summers in the family house. There was not much to do in Aspen. We used the links, we galloped over the sandy roads, we also trotted our several hobbies, Donald, Walter, and I. Sweetheart had no hobby; to make up for this, however, she owned a magnificent team of bêtes-noires—Algebra and French.

As for me, my butterfly collection languished. I had specimens of nearly every butterfly in New York State, and I rather longed for new states to conquer. Anyway, there were plenty of Aspen beauties—I mean the butterflies—flying about the roads and balm-of-Gilead trees, and perhaps that is why I lingered there long enough to collect hundreds of duplicates for exchange. And perhaps it wasn't.

I thought of these things as I sat in the sun-flecked arbour, watching the yellow elm leaves flutter down from the branches. I thought, too, of Sweetheart, and wondered how she would look with her hair up. And while I sat there smoking, watching the yellow leaves drifting across the lawn, a sharp explosion startled me and I raised my head.

Sweetheart was standing on the lawn, gazing dreamily at the smoking débris of a large firecracker.

" What's that for? " I asked.

" It proclaims my independence," said Sweetheart—" my independence forever. Hereafter my cousins will ask to accompany me on my walks; they need no longer charitably permit me to accompany them. Are you three boys going to ride your hobbies? "

" We are," I said.

" Then good-bye. I am going to walk."

" Can't we come too? " I asked, laughing.

" Oh," she said graciously, " if you put it in that way I could not refuse."

" May we bring our guns? " asked Donald from the piazza.

" May I bring my net? " I added, half amused, half annoyed.

She made a gesture, indifferent, condescending.

" Dear me! " murmured the aunts in chorus from the piazza as we trooped after the Aspen beauty, " Sweetheart is growing very fast."

I smiled vaguely at Sweetheart. I was wondering how she would look in long frocks and coiled hair.

II.

In the fall of the year the meadows of Aspen glimmer in the sunlight like crumpled sheets of beaten gold; for Aspen is the land of golden-rod, of yellow earth and gilded fern.

There the crisp oaks rustle, every leaf a blot of yellow; there the burnished pines sound, sound, tremble, and resound, like gilt-stringed harps aquiver in the wind.

Sweet fern, sun-dried, bronzed, fills all the hills with incense, vague and delicate as the white down drifting from the frothy milkweed.

And where the meadow brook prattled, limpid, filtered with sunlight, Sweetheart stood knee-deep in fragrant mint, watching the aimless minnows swimming in circles. On a distant hill, dark against the blue, Donald moved with his dogs, and I saw the sun-glint on his gun, and I heard the distant " Hi—on! Hi— on! " long after he disappeared below the brown hill's brow.

Walter, too, had gone, leaving us there by the brook together, Sweetheart and I; and I saw the crows flapping and circling far over the woods, and I heard the soft report of his dust-shot shells among the trees.

" The ruling passion, Sweetheart," I said. " Donny chases the phantom of pleasure with his dogs. The phantom flies from Walter, and he follows with his dust-shot."

" Then," said Sweetheart, " follow your phantom also; there are butterflies every where." She raised both arms and turned from the brook. " Everywhere flying I see butterflies—phantoms of pleasure; and, Jack, you do not follow with your net."

" No," said I, " the world to-day is too fair to—slay in. I even doubt that the happiness of empires hinges on the discovery of a new species of anything. Do I bore you? "

" A little," said Sweetheart, touching the powdered gold of the blossoms about her. She laid the tip of her third finger on her lips and then on the golden-rod. " I shall not pick it; the world is too fair to-day," she said. " What are you going to do, Jack? "

" I could doze," I said. " Could you? "

"Yes—if you told me stories."

I contemplated her in silence for a moment. After a while she sat down under an oak and clasped her hands.

"I am growing so old," she sighed, "I no longer take pleasure in childish things—Donald's dogs, Walter's humming birds, your butterflies. Jack?"

"What?"

"Sit down on the grass."

"What for?"

"Because I ask you."

I sat down.

Presently she said: "I am as tall as mamma. Why should I study algebra?"

"Because," I answered evasively.

"Your answer is as rude as though I were twenty, instead of sixteen," said Sweetheart. "If you treat me as a child from this moment, I shall hate you."

"Me—Sweetheart?"

"And that name!—it is good for children and kittens."

I looked at her seriously. "It is good for women, too—when it is time," I said. "I prophesy that one day you will hear it again. As for me, I shall not call you by that name if you dislike it."

"I am a woman—now," she said.

"Oh! at sixteen."

"To-morrow I am to be seventeen."

Presently, looking off at the blue hills, I said: " For a long time I have recognised that that subtle, indefinable attitude—we call it deference—due from men to women is due from us to you. Donny and Walter are slower to accept this. You know what you have been to us as a child; we can't bear to lose you—to meet you in another way—to reckon with you as we reckon with a woman. But it is true: our little Sweetheart has vanished, and—*you* are here! "

The oak leaves began to rustle in the hill winds; the crows cawed from the woods.

" Oui c'est moi," she said at length.

" I shall never call you Sweetheart again," I said, smiling.

" Who knows? " she laughed, and leaned over to pick a blade of wild wheat. She coloured faintly a moment later, and said: " I didn't mean that, Jack."

And so Sweetheart took her first step across that threshold of mystery, the Temple of Idols. And of the gilded idols within the temple, one shall turn to living flesh at the sound of a voice. And lo! where a child had entered, a woman returned with the key to the Temple of Gilded Idols.

" Jack," said Sweetheart, " you are wrong. No day is too fair to kill in. I shall pick my arms full—full of flowers."

Over the yellow fields, red with the stalks

of the buckwheat, crowned with a glimmering
cloud of the dusty gold of the golden-rod,
Sweetheart passed, pensive, sedate, awed by the
burden of sixteen years.

I followed.

Over the curling fern and wind-stirred
grasses the silken milkweed seeds sailed, sailed,
and the great red-brown butterflies drifted
above, ruddy as autumn leaves aglow in the sun.

On the sand-cliff there are marigolds," said
Sweetheart.

I looked at the mass of wild flowers in her
arms; her white polished skin reflected the
blaze of colour, warming like ivory under their
glow.

"Marigolds," I repeated; "we will get
some."

"The sand slides on the face of the cliff;
you must be careful," she said.

"And I may see one of those rare cliff butterflies. I haven't any good examples."

I fancy she was not listening; the crows
were clamouring above the beech woods; the
hill winds filled our ears with a sound like the
sound of the sea on shoals. Her gray eyes,
touched with the sky's deep blue and the blue
of the misty hills, looked out across the miles of
woods and fields, and saw a world; not a world
old, scarred, rock-ribbed, and salt with tears,
but a new world, youthful, ripe, sunny, hazy
with the splendour of wonders hidden behind

the horizon—a world jewelled with gems, spanned by rose-mist rainbows—a world of sixteen years.

"We are already at the cliff's edge," I said.

She stepped to the edge and looked over. I drew her back. The sand started among the rocks, running, running with a sound like silver water.

"Then you shall not go either," she said. "I do not care for marigolds."

But I was already on the edge, stooping for a blossom. The next instant I fell.

There was a whistle of sand, a flurry and a rush of wind, a blur of rock, fern, dead grasses —a cry!

For I remember as I fell, falling I called, "Sweetheart!" and again "Sweetheart!" Then my body struck the rocks below.

III.

Of all the seconds that tick the whole year through, of all the seconds that have slipped onward marking the beat of time since time was loosed, there is one, one brief moment, steeped in magic and heavy with oblivion, that sometimes lingers in the soul of man, annihilating space and time. If, at the feet of God, a year is a second passed unnoted, this magic second, afloat on the tide of time, moves on and on till, caught in the vortex of some life's whirl, it sinks into the soul of a being near to death.

And in that soul the magic second glows and lingers, stretching into minutes, hours, days—aye, days and days, till, if the magic hold, the calm years crowd on one by one; and yet it all is but a second—that magic moment that comes on the tide of time—that came to me and was caught up in my life's whirl as I fell, dropping there between sky and earth.

And so that magic moment grew to minutes, to hours; and when my body, whirling, pitching, struck and lay flung out on the earth, the magic second grew until the crystal days fell from my life, as beads, one by one, fall from the rosaries that saints tell kneeling.

Those days of a life that I have lived, those years that linger still aglow in the sun behind me, dim yet splendid as dust-dimmed jewels, they also have ended, not in vague night, but in the sunburst of another second—such a second as ticks from my watch as I write, quick, sharp, joyous, irrevocable! So, of that magic second, or day, or year, I shall tell—I, as I was, standing beside my body flung there across the earth.

I looked at my body, lying in a heap, then turned to the sand cliff smiling.

" Sweetheart! " I called.

But she was already at my side.

We walked on through fragrant pastures, watching the long shadows stretch from field

to field, speaking of what had been and of all
that was to be. It was so simple—everything
was clear before us. Had there been doubts,
fears, sudden alarms, startled heartbeats?

If there had been, now they were ended forever.

"Not forever," said Sweetheart; "who
knows how long the magic second may last?"

"But we—what difference can that make?"
I asked.

"To us?"

"Yes."

"None," said Sweetheart decisively.

We looked out into the west. The sun
turned to a mound of cinders; the hills loomed
in opalescent steam.

"But—but—your shadow!" said Sweetheart.

I bent my head, thrilled with happiness.

"And yours," I whispered.

The shadows we cast were whiter than snow.

I still heard the hill winds, soft in my ears
as breaking surf; a bird-note came from the
dusky woodland; a star broke out overhead.

"What is your pleasure, Sweetheart, now all
is said?" I asked.

"The world is all so fair," she sighed; "is
it fairer beyond the hills, Jack?"

"It is fair where you pass by, north, south,
and from west to west again. In France the
poplars are as yellow as our oaks. In Morbi-

han the gorse gilds all the hills, yellow as golden-rod. Shall we go?"

"But in the spring—let us wait until spring."

"Where?"

"Here."

"Until spring?"

"It is written that Time shall pass as a shadow across the sea. What is that book there under your feet—that iron-bound book, half embedded like a stone in the grass."

"I did not see it!"

"Bring it to me."

I raised the book; it left a bare mark in the sod as a stone that is turned. Then, holding it on my knees, I opened it, and Sweetheart, leaning on my shoulder, read. The tall stars flared like candles, flooding the page with diamond light; the earth, perfumed with blossoms, stirred with the vague vibration of countless sounds, tiny voices swaying breathless in the hidden surge of an endless harmony.

"The white shadow is the shadow of the soul," she read. Even the winds were hushed as her sweet lips moved.

"And what shall make thee to understand what hell is? . . . When the sun shall be folded up as a garment that is laid away; when the stars fall, and the seas boil, and when souls shall be joined again to their bodies; and when the girl who hath been buried alive shall be asked for what crime; when books shall be laid open, when hell shall burn fiercely, and when paradise shall be brought very near:

"Every soul shall know what it hath wrought!"

I closed my eyes; the splendour of the starlight on the page was more than my eyes could bear.

But she read on; for what can dim her eyes?

"O man, verily, labouring, thou labourest to meet thy LORD.

"And thou shalt meet HIM!"

"When the earth shall be stretched like a skin, and shall cast forth that which is therein;

"By the heaven adorned with signs, by the witness and the witnessed;

"By that which appeareth by night; by the daybreak and the ten nights—the ten nights;

"The night of Al Kadr is better than a thousand months.

"Praise be to God, the Lord of all creatures; the Most Merciful, the King of the Day of Judgment. Thee do we worship, and of thee do we beg assistance. Direct us in the right way, in the way of those to whom thou hast been gracious; not of those against whom thou art incensed, nor of those who go astray!"

.   .   .   .

In the sudden silence that spread across earth and heaven I heard the sound of a voice under the earth, calling, calling, calling.

"It is already spring," said Sweetheart; and she rose, placing her white hands in mine. "Shall we go?"

"But we are already there," I stammered, turning my eyes fearfully; for the tall pines dwindled and clustered and rose again cool and gray in the morning air, all turned to stone, fretted and carved like lacework; and where the pines had faded, the twin towers of a cathedral loomed; and where the hills swept across the horizon, the roofs of a white city glimmered in the morning sun. Bridges and quays and streets and domes and the hum of traffic and rattle of arms; and over all, the veil of haze and the twin gray towers of Notre Dame!

"Sweetheart!" I faltered.

But we were already in my studio.

IV.

The studio had not changed. The sun flooded it.

Sweetheart sat in the broken armchair and watched me struggle with the packing. Every now and then she made an impulsive movement toward the heap of clothes on the floor, which I checked with a "Thanks! I can fix it all alone, Sweetheart."

Clifford seemed to extract amusement from it all, and said as much to Rowden, who was as

usual ruining my zitherine by trying to play it
like a banjo.

Elliott, knowing he could be of no use to
us, had the decency to sit outside the studio
on one of the garden benches. He appeared
at intervals at the studio door, saying, " Come
along, Clifford; they don't want you messing
about.   Drop that banjo, Rowden, or Jack will
break your head with it—won't you, Jack? "

I said I would, but not with the zitherine.

Clifford flatly refused to move unless Sweetheart would take him out into our garden and
show him the solitary goldfish which lurked
in the fountain under the almond trees.   But
Sweetheart, apparently fascinated by the mysteries of packing, turned a deaf ear to Clifford's
blandishments and Rowden's discords.

" I imagined," said Clifford, somewhat hurt,
" that you would delight in taking upon yourself the duties of a hostess.   I should be pleased
to believe that I am not an unwelcome guest."

" So should I," echoed Rowden; " I'd be
pleased too."

" What a shame for you to bother, Jack!
she said.   " Mr. Clifford shall go and make some
tea directly.   Mr. Rowden, you may take a
table out by the fountain—and stay there."

Clifford, motioning Elliott to take the other
end of the Japanese table, backed with it
through the hallway and out to the gravel walk,
expostulating.

" The sugar is there in that tin box by the model stand," she said, when he reappeared, " and the extra spoons are lying in a long box on Jack's big easel."

When Rowden, reluctantly relinquishing the zitherine, followed Clifford, bearing the cups and alcohol lamp, I raised my head and wiped the dust from my forehead. I believe I swore a little in French. Sweetheart looked startled. She knew more French than I supposed she did.

" What is it, Jack? "

" Mais—rien, ça m'embête—cette espèce de malle——"

" Then why won't you let me help you, Jack? I can at least put in my gowns."

" But I must pack my colour box first, and the gun case, and the box of reels, and the pastel case, and our shooting boots, and the water-colour box, and the cartridge belt, and your golf shoes, and——"

" O dear! " said Sweetheart with a shudder.

I stood up and scowled at the trunk.

" To look at you, Jack," murmured Sweetheart, " one might think you unhappy."

Unhappy! At the thought our eyes met across the table.

" Unhappy! " I whispered.

Then Clifford came stumbling in, wearing a pair of Joseph's sabots, and, imitating that faithful domestic in voice and manner, in-

vited us to tea under the lilacs and almond
blossoms.

"In a moment," cried Sweetheart impatiently. "Go and pour the tea."

Clifford looked aghast. "No, no!" he
cried; "it's impossible—I won't believe that
you two are deliberately getting rid of me so
you can be alone to spoon! And your honeymoon already a year old, and——"

Sweetheart frowned, and tapped her foot.

Clifford retired indignant.

Then she raised her eyes to mine, and a delicate colour stained her cheeks and neck.

"Yes," I said, "we have been married nearly
a year, Sweetheart."

We looked at our white shadows on the
floor.

v.

Sweetheart sat under the lilac blossoms
pouring out tea for Clifford, Elliott, and Rowden. She was gracious to Clifford, gentle to
Elliott, and she took Rowden under her wing
in the sweetest way possible, to which Clifford
stated his objections.

"Mr. Rowden is younger than you are," she
said gravely. "Monsieur Clifford, I do not
wish you to torment him."

"Rowden's no baby; he's as old as Jack is,
and Jack doesn't murder music."

"I am glad to see you acknowledge Jack's

superiority in all matters," said Sweetheart with a dangerous smile.

"I don't," cried Clifford laughing; "and I don't see what you find to care about in a man who clips his hair like a gendarme and paints everything purple."

"Everything is purple—if Jack paints it so," said Sweetheart, smiling at her reflected face in the water. She stood at the rim of the little stone fountain with her hands clasped behind her back. Elliott and Clifford were poking about in the water plants to dislodge the solitary goldfish, while Rowden gathered dewy clusters of lilacs as an offering.

"There he goes!" said Elliott.

"Poor fellow, living there all alone!" said Sweetheart. "Jack must leave word with Joseph to get him a little lady fish to pay his court to."

"Better put in another gentleman fish, then, if you're following Nature," said Clifford, with an attempt at cynicism which drew the merriest laugh from Sweetheart.

"Oh, how funny is Monsieur Clifford when he wants to be like Frenchmen!" she murmured.

"Jack," said Elliott, as I came from the studio and picked up a cup of tea grown cold, "Clifford's doing the world-worn disenchanted roué."

"And—and I fear he will next make love to me!" cried Sweetheart.

"You'd better look out, Jack," said Clifford darkly, and pretended to sulk until Sweetheart sent him off to buy the bonbons she would need for the train.

"They're packed," I said, "every trunk of them!"

Sweetheart was enchanted. "All my new gowns, and the shoes from Rix's—O Jack, you didn't forget the shoes—and the bath robes—and——"

"All packed," I said, swallowing the tea with a wry face.

"Oh," she cried reproachfully, "don't drink that! Here, I will have some hot tea in a moment," and she ran over and perched on the arm of the garden bench while I lighted the alcohol lamp and then a cigarette.

Rowden came up with his offering of lilacs, and she decorated each of us with a spray.

It was growing late. The long shadows fell across the gravel walks and flecked the white walls of the sculptor's studio opposite.

"It's the nine-o'clock train, isn't it?" said Elliott.

"We will meet you at the station at eight-thirty," added Rowden.

"You don't mind, do you, our dining alone?" said Sweetheart shyly; "it's our last day—Jack's and mine—in the old studio."

"Not the last, I hope," said Elliott sincerely.

We all sat silent for a moment.

"O Paris, Paris—how I fear it!" murmured Sweetheart to me; and in the same breath, "No, no, we must love it, you and I."

Then Elliott said aloud, "I suppose you have no idea when you will return?"

"No," I replied, thinking of the magic second that had become a year.

And so we dined alone, Sweetheart and I, in the old studio.

At half-past eight o'clock the cab stood at the gate with all our traps piled on top, and Joseph and his wife and the two brats were crying, "Au revoir, madame! au revoir, monsieur! We will keep the studio well dusted. Bon voyage! bon voyage!" and all of a sudden my arm was caught by Sweetheart's little gloved hand, and she drew me back through the long ivy-covered alley to the garden where the studio stood, its doorway closed and silent, the hollow windows black and grim. Truly the light had passed away with the passing of Sweetheart. Her hand slipped from my arm, and she went and knelt down at the threshold and kissed it.

"I first knew happiness when I first crossed it," she said; "it breaks my heart to leave it. Only that magic second! but it seems years that we have lived here."

"It was you who brought happiness to it," I said.

"Good-bye! good-bye, dear, dear, old studio!" she cried. "Oh, if Jack is always the same to me as he has been here—if he will be faithful and true in that new home!"

The new home was to be in a strange land. Sweetheart was a little frightened, but was dying to go there. Sweetheart had never seen the golden gorse ablaze on the moors of Morbihan.

VI.

I went inside the brass railing and waited my turn to buy the tickets. When it came, I took two first class to Quimperlé, for it was to be an all-night ride, and there was no sleeping car. Clifford had taken charge of the baggage, and I went with him to have it registered, leaving Sweetheart with Elliott and Rowden. All the traps were there—the big trunks, the big valises, my sketching kit, the zitherine in a leather case, two handbags, a bundle of umbrellas and canes, and a huge package of canvases. The toilet case and the rugs and waterproofs we took with us into the compartment.

The compartment was empty. Sweetheart nestled into one corner, and when I had placed our traps in the racks overhead I sat down opposite, while Clifford handed in our sandwiches, a bottle of red wine, and Sweetheart's box of bonbons.

We didn't say much; most had been said before starting. Clifford was more affected than he cared to show—I know by the way he grasped my hand. They are dear fellows, every one. We did not realize that we were actually going—going, perhaps, forever. She laughed, and chatted, and made fun of Clifford, and teased Rowden, aided and abetted by Elliott, until the starting gong clanged and a warning whistle sounded along the gaslit platform.

"Jack," cried Clifford, leaning in the window, "God bless you! God bless you both!"

Elliott touched her hand and wrung mine, and Rowden risked his neck to give us both one last cordial grasp.

"Count on me—on us," cried Clifford, speaking in English, "if you are—troubled!"

By what, my poor Clifford? Can you, with all your gay courage, turn back the hands of the dials? Can you, with all your warm devotion, add one second to the magic second and make it two? The shadows we cast are white.

The train stole out into the night, and I saw them grouped on the platform, silhouettes in the glare of the yellow signals. I drew in my head and shut the window. Sweetheart's face had grown very serious, but now she smiled across from her corner.

"Aren't you coming over by me, Jack?"

VII.

We must have been moving very swiftly, for the car rocked and trembled, and it was probably that which awoke me. I looked across at Sweetheart. She was lying on her side, one cheek resting on her gloved hand, her travelling cap pushed back, her eyes shut. I smoothed away the curly strands of hair which straggled across her cheeks, and tucked another rug well about her feet. Her feet were small as a child's. I speak as if she were not a child. She was eighteen then.

The next time I awoke we lay in a long gaslit station. Some soldiers were disembarking from the forward carriages, and a gendarme stalked up and down the platform.

I looked sleepily about for the name of the station. It was painted in blue over the buffet— "Petit St. Yves." "Is it possible we are in Brittany?" I thought. Then the voices of the station hands, who were hoisting a small boat upon the forward carriage, settled my doubts. "Allons! tire hardiment, Jean Louis! mets le cannotte deboutte."

Arrête toi Yves! doucement! doucement! Sacré garce!"

Somewhere in the darkness a mellow bell tolled. I settled back to slumber, my eyes on Sweetheart.

She slept.

VIII.

I awoke in a flood of brightest sunshine. From our window I could look into the centre of a most enchanting little town, all built of white limestone and granite. The June sunshine slanted on thatched roof and painted gable, and fairly blazed on the little river slipping by under the stone bridge in the square.

The streets and the square were alive with rosy-faced women in white head-dresses. Everywhere the constant motion of blue skirts and spotless coiffes, the twinkle of varnished socks, the clump! clump! of sabots.

Like a black shadow a priest stole across the square. Above him the cross on the church glowed like a live cinder, flashing its reflection along the purple-slated roof from the eaves of which a cloud of ash-gray pigeons drifted into the gutter below. I turned from the window to encounter Sweetheart's eyes. Her lips moved a little, her long lashes heavy with slumber drooped lower, then with a little sigh she sat bolt upright. When I laughed, as I always did, she smiled, a little confused, a little ashamed, murmuring: "Bonjour, mon chéri! Quelle heure est-il?" That was always the way Sweetheart awoke.

"O dear, I am so rumpled!" she said. "Jack, get me the satchel this minute, and don't look at me until I ask you to."

I unlocked the satchel, and then turning to the window again threw it wide open. Oh, how sweet came the morning air from the meadows! Some young fellows below on the bank of the stream were poking long cane fishing-rods under the arches of the bridge.

"Sweetheart," I said over my shoulder, "I believe there are trout in this stream."

"Mr. Elliott says that whenever you see a puddle you always say that," she replied.

"What does he know about it?" I answered, "for I am touchy on the subject; "he doesn't know a catfish from a—a dogfish."

"Neither do I, Jack dear, but I'm going to learn. Don't be cross."

She had finished her toilet and came over to the window, leaning out over my shoulder.

"Where are we?" she cried in startled wonder at the little white town and the acres of swaying clover. "Oh, Jack, is—is this the country?"

A man in uniform passing under our window looked up surprised.

"What are you doing here?" he demanded; then, seeing Sweetheart, he took off his gold-laced cap, and added, with a bow: "This carriage goes no farther, monsieur—madame——"

"Merci!" exclaimed Sweetheart, "we wish to go to Quimperlé!"

"And we have tickets for Quimperlé," I insisted.

"But," smiled the official, "this is Quimperlé."

It was true. There was the name written over the end of the station; and, looking ahead, I saw that our car had been detached and was standing in stately seclusion under the freight shed. How long it had been standing so Heaven alone knows; but they evidently had neglected to call us, and there we were inhabiting a detached carriage in the heart of Quimperlé. I managed to get a couple of porters, and presently we found all our traps piled up on the platform, and a lumbering vehicle with a Breton driver waiting to convey us to the hotel.

"Which," said I to the docile Breton, "is the best hotel in Quimperlé?"

"The Hôtel Lion d'Or," he replied.

"How do you know?" I demanded.

"Because," said he mildly, "it is the only hotel in Quimperlé."

Sweetheart observed that this ought to be convincing, even to me, and she tormented me all the way to the square, where I got even by pretending to be horrified at her dishevelled condition incident to a night's railway ride in a stuffy compartment.

"Don't, Jack! people will look at us."

"Let 'em."

"Oh, this is cruel! Oh, I'll pay you for this!"

And they did look at us—or rather at her; for from the time Sweetheart and I had cast our lots together, I noticed that I seemed to escape the observation of passers-by. When I lived alone in Paris I attracted a fair share of observation from the world as it wagged on its Parisian way. It was pleasant to meet a pretty girl's eyes now and then in the throng which flowed through the park and boulevard. I really never flattered myself that it was because of my personal beauty; but in Paris, any young fellow who is dressed in the manner of Albion, hatted and gloved in the same style, is not entirely a cipher. But now it was not the same, by a long shot.

Sweetheart's beauty simply put me in my place as an unnoticed but perhaps correct supplement to her.

She knew she was a beauty, and was delighted when she looked into her mirror. Nothing escaped her. The soft hair threaded with sunshine, which, when loosened, curled to her knees; the clear white forehead and straight brows; the nose delicate and a trifle upturned; the scarlet lips and fine cut chin—she knew the value of each of these. She was pleased with the soft, full curve of her throat, the little ears, and the colour which came and went in her cheeks.

But her eyes were the first thing one noticed. They were the most beautiful gray eyes that ever opened under silken lashes. She approved of my telling her this, which duty I fulfilled daily. Perhaps it may be superfluous to say that we were very much in love. Did I say *were?*

I think that, as I am chanting the graces of Sweetheart, it might not be amiss to say that she is just an inch shorter than I am, and that no Parisienne carried a pretty gown with more perfection than she did. I have seen gowns that looked like the devil on the manikin, but when Sweetheart wore them they were the astonishment and admiration of myself. And I do know when a woman is well dressed, though I am an art critic.

Sweetheart regarded her beauty as an intimate affair between ourselves, a precious gift for our mutual benefit, to be carefully treasured and petted. Her attitude toward the world was unmistakable. The world might look— she was indifferent. With our intimate friends she was above being flattered. Clifford said to me once: " She carries her beauty as a princess would carry the Koh-i-noor—she knows she is worthy of it, and hopes it is worthy of her.

" We ought to be so happy that I am beautiful! " she would say to me. " Just think, supposing I were not! "

I used to try to make her believe that it would have made no difference.

" Oh, not now," she would say gravely. " I

know that if I lost it it would be the same to us both, now; but you can't make me believe that, at first, when you used to lean over the terrace of the Luxembourg and wait patiently for hours just to see me walk out of the Odeon."

"I didn't," I would always explain; "I was there by accident."

"Oh, what a funny accident to happen every day for two months!"

"Stop teasing! Of course, after the first week———"

"And what a funny accident that I should pass the same way every day for two months, when before I always went by the Rue de Seine!"

There was once such an accident, and such a girl. I never knew her; she is dead. I wondered sometimes that Sweetheart knew, and believed it was she herself. Yet the other woman's shadow was black.

Sweetheart had a most peculiar and unworldly habit of not embellishing facts. She presently displayed it when we arrived at the Hôtel Lion d'Or.

"Jack," said she nervously, "the cinders have made your face unpleasant. I am ashamed. They may not believe you are my husband."

"As monsieur and madame," I said, "we may have dirty faces and be honest."

"Do you suppose they—they will believe it? These queer people———"

"They'd better!" I said fiercely.

"I—I hadn't thought of that," she said.
"You see, in our own little place in Paris everybody knew it, but here——"

I said, "Dearest, what nonsense!" and we
marched unceremoniously up to the register,
where I wrote our names. Then, with a hasty
little squeeze of her gloved hand, she turned to
the maid and tripped off to inspect our quarters.
While I was pumping the fat-headed old proprietor about the trout fishing in the vicinity,
the maid returned with the request that I
mount to the room above. I followed her along
the tiled passages and found Sweetheart sitting
on a trunk.

"It's charming! charming!" she said.
"Just look at the roses outside, and the square,
and the river! and oh, Jack, the funny little
Breton cattle, and the old man with knee-
breeches! It's charming! and"—here she
caught sight of the enraptured and fascinated
maid—"and you are charming, with your red
cheeks and white coiffe," she said. "Oh, how
pretty!"

"Oh, madame!" murmured the servant in
dire confusion.

I said, "Dearest, that will do. Nobody
speaks of my peculiar charms, and I wish to be
noticed."

The presence of the maid prevented Sweetheart from making amends, so we told her we

were satisfied, and we would spare her life if she prepared breakfast in seventeen seconds.

She accepted the gift of existence with a dazed courtsey, and vanished.

It was refreshing to get hold of a sponge and cold water after fourteen hours in a cramped compartment. Hunger drove us to hurry—a thing we rarely did in the morning—and the way we splashed cold water about would have been fatal to any but a tiled floor.

" Dear," I said, " you have not yet seen me in my Tyrolese knickerbockers and beautiful shooting jacket. You have never beheld my legs clothed in Tyrolese stockings, at twenty francs a pair."

" The legs? " she inquired from the depths of a bath robe.

I ignored the question, and parted my hair with care. Then I sat down on the window and whistled.

Of course I was ready first. Sweetheart's hair had got into a tangle and needed to be all combed out.

" Oh, I know you are impatient, because you're whistling the Chant du Départ," she said from the door of her toilet room.

" As usual," I said, " I am ready first."

" If you say that again——" she threatened.

I said it, and dodged a sponge. Presently I was requested to open the trunk and select a gown for her. Dear little Sweetheart! she loved to pretend that she had so many it needed long consultation to decide which.

" The dark blue? " I inquired.

" Don't you think it is too warm? "

" The pale blue, then—or the pink and white? "

" Why not the white, with the cuffs à l'Anglaise, and the canoe hat? "

I hauled it out.

Then, of course, she changed her mind.

" I think the gray is better for the morning; then I can wear the big chip hat."

I fished up the gray. It was light, almost silvery, and had white spots on it.

" Jack, dear," she said, coming out with her hair tucked up in a knot, drawing the bath robe up to her chin with both hands, " I think that the white cloth would be better, and that I can wear the béret."

By this time the trunk was in a pretty mess, which amused her; but at last I ferreted out the white cloth dress, and, refusing to listen to further discussion, sat down on the window seat. Sweetheart enjoyed it.

" Stop telling me to hurry," she said; " I can't, if you keep saying it all the time."

After a while she called me to fasten her corsage, which hooked with about ten hundred hooks along the side and collar. I hated to do it, and my finger ends stung for hours after, but, as Sweetheart very rightly says, " When we are rich enough to have a maid you needn't," I submitted with an air which delighted her. Her tormenting " Thank you, Jack," was the last straw, so I calmly picked her up and carried her out, and almost to the dining room, where I set her down just in time to avoid the proprietor and three domestics issuing from the office.

Sweetheart was half inclined to laugh, half indignant, and wholly scandalized. But she did not dare say anything, for we were at the dining-room door.

There were some people there, but except for a slight inclination we did not notice each other. We had a small table to ourselves by the rose-bowered window.

We were very hungry. Breakfast began with fresh sardines just caught, and ended with little Breton cakes and a demi-tasse. I finished first; I always do, because the wretched habit of bolting my food, contracted while studying under Bouguereau at Julian's, clings to me yet. Oh, I shall have a merry time paying for it when I am forty! I began, as usual, to tease Sweetheart.

" If you continue to eat like this, dear, you will never be able to wear your new frocks. This one seems a trifle too tight now."

Sweetheart, who prided herself as much on her figure as on her lovely face, repelled the insult with disdain and nibbled her Breton bis-

cuit defiantly. When at last she condescended
to rise, we strolled out under the trees in front
of the hotel, and sat down on the low stone wall
surrounding the garden. The noon sun hung
in the zenith, flooding the town with a dazzling
downpour. Sunbeams glanced and danced on
the water; sunbeams filtered through the foli-
age; sunbeams stole under Sweetheart's big
straw hat, searching the depths of the gray eyes.
Sunbeams played merry mischief with my ears
and neck, which were beginning to sting in the
first sunburn of the year. Through the square
the white-coiffed women passed and repassed;
small urchins with silver-buckled hatbands
roamed about the bridge and market-place until
collected and trooped off to school by a black-
robed Jesuit frère; and in the shade of the trees
a dozen sprawling men in Breton costume
smoked their microscopical pipes and watched
the water.

"They are an industrious race," said I
with fine irony, watching a happy inebriate
pursuing a serpentine course toward the café
opposite.

Sweetheart, who was as patriotic a little girl
as ever hummed the Marseillaise, and adopted
France as long as she lived in it, was up in arms
in an instant.

"I have read," she said with conviction,
"that the Bretons are a brave, industrious race.
They are French."

"They speak a different language," I said—
"not a word of French in it."

"They are French," repeated Sweetheart,
with an inflection which decided me to shun the
subject until I could unpack my guide-book.

We sat a little while longer under the trees,
until we both began nodding and mutually ac-
cused each other. Then Sweetheart went up
to the room to take a nap, and I, scorning
such weakness, lay down in a steamer chair
under our window and fell fast asleep in no
time.

I was aroused by a big pink rose which hit
me squarely on the mouth. Sweetheart was
perched in the window seat above, and as I
looked up she sent a shower of blossoms down
upon me.

"Jack, you lazy creature, it's five o'clock,
and I'm dressed and ready for a walk!"

"So am I," I said, jumping up.

"But not like that. You must come up
and make yourself nice for dinner."

"Nice? What's the matter with these
tweeds? Aren't these new stockings present-
able?"

"Look at your hair!" she said evasively.
"Come up this minute and brush it."

I went, and was compelled to climb into a
white collar and shirt, and trousers of an English cut. But before we had gone far along
the great military road that climbed the heights

above the little river, I took Sweetheart's hand in mine and imparted to her my views and intentions upon the subject of my costume for the future.

" You see, dearest, we are here in Brittany for three reasons. The first is, that I should paint outdoors. The second is, that we should economize like the deuce. The third is, our shadows——"

" I know," she interrupted faintly. " Never mind, Jack, dear."

We walked silently for a while, hand clasping hand very tightly, for we were both thinking of the third reason.

I broke the silence first, speaking cheerfully, and she looked up with a quick smile while the shadow fell from her brow.

" You see, dear, in this place, where we are going, there are no people but peasants. Your frocks are all right for a place like this; we must both wear our free-and-easy togs—I for painting, and you for scrambling about after your wild flowers or fishing with me. If you get tired of seeing me in corduroys or tweeds, I'll dress for you when you think you can't stand it any longer."

" Oh, Jack, I do like your knickerbockers——"

" And you shall wear your most gorgeous gown for me——"

" Indeed I won't," she laughed, adding impulsively, "indeed I will—every day, if you wish it!"

At the top of the hill stood an ancient Ursuline convent surrounded by a high wall, which also inclosed the broad acres of the wealthy sisterhood. We sat down by the roadside hedge and looked across the valley, where the hurrying river had ceased to hasten and now lingered in placid pools and long, deep reaches. The sun had set behind the forest, and the sky threw a purple light over woods and meadow. The grassy pools below were swept by flocks of whistling martins and swallows. One or two white gulls flapped slowly toward the tide water below, and a young curlew, speeding high overhead, uttered a lonesome cry. The grass—the brilliant green grass of Brittany—had turned a deep metallic blue in the twilight. A pale primrose light grew and died in the sky, and the forest changed from rose to ashes. Then a dull red bar shot across the parting clouds in the west, the forest smouldered an instant, and the pools glowed crimson. Slowly the red bar melted away, the light died out among the branches, the pools turned sombre. Looking up, we saw the new moon flashing in the sky above our heads. Sweetheart sighed in perfect contentment.

"It's beautiful!" I said, with another sigh.

"Ah, yes," she murmured, "beautiful to

you, and to me—to me, Jack, who have never before seen this land of Morbihan."

After a while she said, "And the ocean—oh, how I long to see it! Is it near us, Jack?"

"The river runs into it twenty kilometres below. We feel the tide at Quimperlé." I did not add, "Baedeker."

"I wonder," I said presently, "what are the feelings of a little American who sees this country—the real country—for the first time?"

"I suppose you mean me," she said. "I don't know—I don't think I understand it yet, but I know I shall love it, and never want to go back."

"Perhaps we never shall," I said. "The magic second may stretch into years that end at last as all ends."

Then our hands met in that sudden nervous clasp which seemed to help and steady us when we were thinking of the real world, so long, so long forgotten.

IX.

I was awakened next morning by a spongeful of cold water in the face, which I hate. I started up to wreak vengeance upon Sweetheart, but she fled to the toilet room and locked herself in. From this retreat she taunted me until further sleep was out of the question, and I

bowed to the inevitable—indignantly, when I
saw my watch pointed to five o'clock.

Sweetheart was perfectly possessed to row;
so when I had bolted my coffee and sat watching her placidly sip hers, we decided to go
down to the bank of the little stream and hire
a boat. The boat was a wretched, shapeless
affair, with two enormous oars and the rem-
nants of rowlocks. It was the best boat in
town, so we took it. I managed to get away
from the bank, and, conscious of Sweetheart's
open admiration, pulled boldly down the stream.
It was easy work, for the tide was ebbing. The
river up to the bridge was tidal, but above the
bridge it leaped and flowed, a regular salmon
stream. Sweetheart was so impatient to take
the oars that I relinquished them and picked
up my rod. The boat swung down the stream
and under the high stone viaduct, where I insisted on anchoring and whipping the promising-looking water. The water was likely
enough, and the sudden splash of a leaping
grilse added to its likelihood. I was in hopes
a grilse might become entangled with one of
the flies, but though a big one shot up out of the
water within five feet of Sweetheart, causing
her to utter a suppressed scream, neither grilse
nor trout rose to the beautiful lures I trailed
about, and I only hooked two or three enormous
dace, which came up like logs and covered the
bottom of the boat with their coarse scales.

Sweetheart had never seen a French trout uncooked, and scarcely shared my disappointment.

"They are splendid fish," she repeated; "you are unreasonable."

There was an ancient Breton squatting on the bank; from his sulky attitude I took him to be a poacher visiting his infernal set lines and snares; but I hailed him pleasantly with a bonjour, which he returned civilly enough.

"Are there trout in this stream?"

"About the bridge," he replied cautiously.

"Have you caught any?"

"I ain't fishing," he said, much alarmed.

"What's that?" I demanded, pointing to as plump a trout as ever I saw, floating on the end of a string under the bank.

"Where?" he asked, looking about him with affected concern.

"There!"

He looked around, everywhere except where I pointed. He examined the horizon, and the tree tops, as though he expected a fish on every twig. I poled the boat up to the bank and pointed out the fish.

"Ma doui!" he exclaimed, "there *is* a fish!"

"Yes, a trout," I said.

"Trout?" He burst into a forced laugh. "Trout! Ha! ha! Why, monsieur, that is a dace—a poor little dace!" He hastily jerked it up with a long homemade gaff which lay—of course quite by accident—at his feet.

"A poor little dace!" he mumbled. "Of course, monsieur would not care to claim such a poor, coarse little fish; but I am only too glad to eat it—ah, yes, only too glad!"

"You see," said Sweetheart impulsively, "that you are wrong. Give him our fish; that will make four dace for the poor fellow."

I placed the three dace across the blade of my oar and held it out to the poacher. He took them as if he were really glad to get them. Then I said, "These are dace, and they don't have red spots."

He stood as if ready to bolt, but I laughed, and settled back on my oars, saying: "You're a poacher; but I don't care a continental, and you can poach all day in this confounded country, where there is about one trout to the kilometre. Don't look scared. What do I care? Only don't tell me I'm unable to distinguish a trout when I can see the tip of his nose."

I then sailed majestically out into the stream.

Sweetheart wanted to know whether that was really a real poacher. She had read about them. Her ideal poacher was a young, stalwart, eagle-eyed giant, with a tangle of hair and a disposition toward assassination. The reality shocked her.

"Anyway," she said, "you frightened the poor old thing. How rough men are!"

We returned to the landing place with difficulty, for the tide was still on the ebb, and we got aground more than once. My hands were in a fine condition when at last I drove that wretched scow into the mud and lifted Sweetheart out to the firm bank. The evil-eyed old man who rented us the boat glanced sardonically at my rod and blistered hands, and I was glad enough to pay him all he asked and break away for the hotel.

We had an hour to lunch in, pack, and be ready for the trap which was to bear us to our destination—the distant village of Faöuet, in Morbihan.

X.

A long drive on a smooth white road, acres of gorse and broom, beech woods and oak thickets, and the "Heu! heu! Allo! Allons! en route!" of the Breton driver, these are my recollections of the ride to Faöuet. There are others, too—the hedges heavy with bloom, the perfume of the wild honeysuckle, the continual bird chorus from every grove and every bramble patch—and Sweetheart's veil flying into my face.

We have spoken of it since together, but she has few recollections of that journey. She only remembers it as her first steps into our heritage.

And so we entered into our heritage, Sweetheart and I; and our heritage was very fair, for it lay everywhere about us. It was a world which we alone inhabited. Men said, "This land is Gloanec's," "This is Gurnalec's," "This is Kerdec's"; they spoke of "my woods" and "his meadows" and "their pastures." And how we laughed; for when we passed together through their lands, around us, far as the eye could reach, our heritage lay in the sunshine.

XI.

One day, when Sweetheart had been weeping—for we were thinking of the end to the magic second—I spoke of our heritage which swept far as the eye could reach across the moors of Faöuet.

She said: "The past is ours, Jack; the present is ours; the future——"

We tried to smile, but our hearts were like lead. Yet we know that the future will also be ours. I know it as I write.

XII.

The letter from St. Gildas, bringing with it a breath of salt air, lay on the table before us. Sweetheart clasped her hands and looked at me.

"I'm in favour of going at once," I said for the third time. Over by the wall were piled my canvases, the result of three months in Faöuet.

The first was a study of Sweetheart under the trees of the ancient orchard in the convent grounds. What trouble I had had with that canvas! I remembered the morning that the old gardener came over and stood behind me as I painted; and when I had replied to his "Good-morning," I recalled the pang his next words gave me:

"I am so sorry, monsieur, but it is forbidden to enter the convent grounds."

My canvas was almost finished, and, as the romancers have it, "my despair was great!" A month's work for nothing—or next to nothing!

Sweetheart rose from her pose on the low bough of the apple tree and came over to my side. "Never mind, Jack; I shall go and ask the Mother Superior about it."

I knew that she would win over the Mother Superior; and when, that evening, she came back radiant, crying, "She is lovely!—she says you may finish the picture, and I think you ought to go and thank her," I put on my cap, and stepping across the street, we rang at the gate.

The old gardener let us in, and in a moment I stood before the latticed windows behind which some one was moving. In a low voice the invisible nun told us that the Superior granted to us the privilege of working in the orchard, but we must be careful of the grass, because it was almost time to cut it.

"I am sure we may have confidence in you," she said.

"We will not trample the grass, my sister, and I thank you for us both."

The lattice trembled, was raised a little, and then fell.

"You are English," said the hidden nun.

"I am American, my sister."

I looked at the lattice a moment, then dropped my eyes. I may have been mistaken, but I think she sighed.

Sweetheart came closer to the lattice and murmured her thanks.

There was a pause.

Then came the voice again, sweet and gentle: "May Our Lady of Saint Gildas protect you"; and we went out by the little iron wicket.

The next picture was another study of Sweetheart in the woods; the next, another study of Sweetheart; and the others were studies of the same young lady.

The light in the room had grown dim, and I walked to the window which overlooked the convent chapel. The chapel windows were open; within, the nuns stood or knelt chanting. Three white-veiled figures were advancing to the altar, and the others, draped in black now knelt behind. I didn't think I had any business to look at them, so I did not. After all, they were cloistered nuns, and it was only on hot nights that they opened the chapel windows. Sweetheart was speaking beside my shoulder.

"Poor things! The ones in white, they are the novices; they will never see parents or friends again. When they enter the gates they never leave—never; they are buried there."

I said: "After all, we are much like them. We have left all; we have nothing now but each other, for the world is dead, and we are bound by vows which keep us within the narrow confines of our heritage."

"But our heritage is everywhere—as far as we can see."

"Ah, yes, but we can only see to the horizon. There is a world beyond."

"I have renounced it," said Sweetheart faintly.

XIII.

The letter from St. Gildas had been lying on our table for a week before I thought of answering it, and even then it was Sweetheart who wrote:

" DEAR MR. STUART:

" Jack is too lazy to answer your kind note, so, in pure shame for his discourtesy, I hasten to reply to your questions.

" First: Yes; we have been working very hard, and Jack's pictures are charming, though he growls over them all day.

" Second: Yes; we intend to stay in Brittany this winter for lots of reasons—one being economy, and another, Jack's outdoor painting.

" Third: Yes; we are coming to St. Gildas.

" Fourth: To-morrow.

" Fifth: No; we had not heard of Mr. Clifford's affair with the policeman; and oh, I am so sorry he was locked up and fined! Jack laughs. I suspect he, too, was as wicked as you all when he was a student, alone in Paris.

" Sixth: I know you are Jack's oldest and most intimate friend, so I allow you more liberty than I do Messieurs Clifford and Elliott; therefore I will answer your question as to whether the honeymoon is not on the wane. No! no! no! There are three answers to one question. See how generous I can be! "

Sweetheart called me to see whether or not I approved. I did, and added my answer to Stuart's last question as follows: " No, you idiot! " Then I signed the note, and Sweetheart sealed and directed it.

So we left for St. Gildas next morning before sunrise and in the rain. This leaving at such an unearthly hour was not my doing, but Sweetheart was determined, and rose by candlelight in spite of desperate opposition on my part. It was cold, and the rain beat against the windows.

It was many kilometres to St. Gildas, but before we had gone six, the rain had ceased and the eastern sky flushed to a pale rose.

" Thank goodness! " I said, " we shall have the sun."

Then the daily repeated miracle of the coming of dawn was wrought before our eyes. The heavens glowed in rainbow tints; the shredded mist rising along the river was touched with purple and gold, and acres of meadow and pasture dripped precious stones. Shreds of the fading night-mist drifted among the tree tops, now tipped with fire, while in the forest depths faint sparkles came from some lost ray of morning light falling on wet leaves. Then of a sudden up shot the sun, and against it, black and gigantic, a peasant towered, leaning upon his spade.

XIV.

We were fast nearing the end of our long journey. The sun blazed on us from the zenith, and the wheels creaked with the heat of the white road. The driver leaned back, say-

ing, " We enter Finistère here by this granite
post." Presently he added, " The ocean! "

There it lay, a basin of silver and blue.
Sweetheart had started to her feet, speechless,
one hand holding to my shoulder, the other
clasped to her breast. And now, as the road
wound through the hills and down to the coast,
long stretches of white sand skirted the distant
cliffs, and over the cliffs waved miles and miles
of yellow gorse. A cluster of white and gray
houses lay in the hollow to the left almost at
the mouth of the river, and beyond, the waves
were beating in the bar—beating the same
rhythm which we were to hear so long there
together, day and night. There was not a boat
to be seen, not a creature, nor was there any
sign of life save for the smoke curling from
a cottage chimney below. The ocean lay
sparkling beneath, and beyond its deeper blue
melted into the haze on the horizon.

Suddenly, in the road below, the figure of a
man appeared, and at the same moment a
pointer pup came gambolling up beside us in
an ecstasy of self-abnegation and apology. I
sprang out of the lumbering vehicle and lifted
Sweetheart to the ground, and in an instant we
were shaking hands with a stalwart young fellow in knickerbockers and jersey, who said we
were a pretty pair not to have come sooner,
and told Sweetheart he pitied her lot—meaning
me.

Then we walked arm in arm down a fragrant lane to the river bank, where the dearest old lady toddled out of the granite house to welcome us and show us our rooms. Sweetheart went with her, while I stopped an instant to chat with Stuart.

"That is Madame Ylven," he said. "She is the most stunning peasant woman in Finistère, and you will want for nothing." Then, after a moment, "Good heavens! Jack, what a beauty your wife——" He stopped short, but added, "What a delicious little beauty Sweetheart has grown to be!"

A white-coiffed maid came to the door, and said, "Will monsieur have the goodness to come? Madame wishes him to see the rooms."

The wind blew from the south, and the thunder of the sea was in my ears as I mounted the stairs to our new quarters.

Sweetheart met me at the door, saying, "It seems almost too much happiness to bear, but I feel that we are at home at last—alone together for all time."

Alone together? The ocean at our threshold, the moors and forests at our back, and a good slate roof above us. Before me through the open door I could see the great old-fashioned room, warm in the afternoon sunlight— the room we were to live in so long, the room in which we were to pass the happiest and bitterest moments of our lives.

She hesitated an instant before the threshold. I think we knew that we stood upon the threshold of our destiny. Then I said, half in earnest: "Are you afraid to cross with me into the unknown future? See, the room is filled with sunshine. Are you afraid?"

She sprang across the threshold, and, turning to me, held out both hands.

XV.

The sun slipped lower and lower into the sea, until a distant tossing wave washed it out against the sky. Light died in the room, and shadows closed around us; yet it was in the darkness and shadows that we drew nearer to each other, then and after.

XVI.

Stuart stood under our window and yelled up at me, "Oh, Jack! I say, Jack!"

Sweetheart, who was fussing over the half-unpacked trunk, went to the window and threw open the panes.

"You don't mean to say you have had your coffee?" she said. "Jack isn't up yet."

"Jack is up," I explained, coming to the window in pajamas. "Hello!"

"I only wanted to say that I haven't had my coffee," he explained, "and I'm going to take it with you when you're ready."

Sweetheart picked up her béret, and, passing a hatpin through it, turned to me with a warning, "I shall eat all the breakfast, monsieur!" and vanished down the stairs. A moment later I heard her clear voice below:

> Sonnez le chœur,
> Chasseur!
> Sonnez la mort!

Before I had finished dressing, Sweetheart tripped in with my coffee and toast.

"Of course I've finished," she said, "and you don't deserve this. Mr. Stuart has gone off with his canvases, and says he'll see you at lunch."

I swallowed the coffee and browsed on little squares of toast which she condescendingly buttered for me, and then, lighting a cigarette, I announced my intention of commanding an exploring expedition consisting of Sweetheart and myself. A scratching at the door and a patter of feet announced that I had been overheard.

Sweetheart unlatched the door, and the pointer pup of the evening before charged into the room and covered us with boisterous caresses, which we took to indicate that he not only approved of the expedition, but intended to undertake the general supervision of it himself. I resigned the leadership at once.

"His name," said Sweetheart in the tone

of one who presents a distinguished guest, " is ' Luff.' "

I gravely acknowledged the honour by patting his head.

" I'm afraid," I said to Sweetheart, " that there is a bar sinister upon his escutcheon, but possibly it is only the indelible mark of the conquering British foxhound."

Sweetheart said, " Nonsense! " and the expedition moved, Luff leading with a series of ear-splitting orders in the dog language which we perfectly understood.

In ten minutes we stood on the cliffs, the salt wind whipping our faces. Saint-Gildas-des-Prés lay at our feet.

" I know," observed Sweetheart calmly, " all about this place. Captain Ylven told me at breakfast."

" Well," said I, " what's that island on the horizon? "

Then she overwhelmed me with erudition, until I longed for Baedeker and revenge.

" That is the Isle de Groix, and all about us is the Bay of Biscay. This little hamlet on the cliff is St. Julien, and if we follow the coast far enough we come to Lorient."

" Follow the coast? Which way? "

Sweetheart had forgotten, and I triumphed in silence, until she stamped her foot and marched off to assist Luff in investigating a suspicious hole in the cliff.

I went to the edge of the plateau and looked over. The surf thundered against the rocks, tossing long strands of seaweed over the pebbly beach. A man with a wooden rake stood in the water up to his knees. He raked the seaweed from the breakers as a farmer rakes weeds from the lawn. The salt wind began to sting my lips and eyes. My throat felt dry and salty. I turned toward the hamlet of St. Gildas. I had not imagined it so small. Besides our house there were but three others clustered under the river bank. Behind it stretched woods and grain fields broken by patches of yellow gorse. Across the river stood a stone chapel almost lost in the miles of moorland. To the east and west the downs covered with gorse and heather rolled to the horizon. Here and there along the cliffs stood what appeared to be the ruins of ancient forts, and on a rock, just where the river sweeps out into the sea, rose a dirty white signal tower. The tower was low and squatty and wet. It looked like some saline excrescence which had slowly exuded from the brine-soaked rock. On the bar hundreds of white gulls rose and settled as the tide encroached; curlew were running along the foam-splashed shore under the eastern cliffs across the river.

On our side of the river the cliffs were covered with blackthorn and hawthorn, with here and there a stunted oak, probably so placed by Providence as general rendezvous for all the small twittering birds of Finistère. Birds were everywhere. From the clouds came the ceaseless carol of skylarks; from the grain fields and the flowering gorse rose an unbroken chorus, taken up and repeated by flocks of microscopical songsters among the blackthorns on the cliffs.

"This is paradise, this wilderness," I thought.

Then, as I heard Sweetheart's mocking voice from the cliff:

> O frère Jaques,
> Dormez vous!

"I'm not asleep!" I cried in answer. "What is it?"

"Luff has unearthed a poor little mole, but I won't allow him to hurt it."

"Jack, dear," she said, as I came up, "couldn't we keep it as a pet? See, the poor little thing is blind."

As it was blind we called it "Love," which later was changed to "Cupid," and finally, when we discovered it true gormandizing character, for "Cupid" we substituted "Cupidity," by which name it flourished and fattened.

"What a change," said Sweetheart sadly, "from Blind Love to Blind Greed!"

The mole grew very fat.

XVII.

When the winds stir the leaves among the poplars, and the long shadows fall athwart the fields; when the winds rise at night, and the branches scrape and crack above the moonlit snow; when in the long hot days the earth is bathed in fragrance, and all the little creatures of the fields are silent; when in the still evenings the flowers perfume the air, and the gravel walks shine white in the moonlight; when the breezes quicken from the distant coast; when the sand shakes beneath the shock of the breakers, and every wave is plumed with white; when the calm eye of the beacon turns to mine, lingers, and turn away, and the surf is yeasty and thick; when I start at the sound of a voice from the cliffs, and my eyes are raised in vain; when the white gulls toss and drift in the storm-clouds, and the water hurries out in the black ebb tide; when I rise and look from the window; when I dress; when I work with pen and colour; when I rest; when I walk; when I sleep—there is one face before my eyes, one name on my lips. For the white shadow is turning gray, and God alone knows the end.

XVIII.

And God alone knows the end, for the mists are crowding, brooding like angry-browed clouds, and I hear the whistle of unseen winds, and my life-flame wavers and sinks and flares, blown hither and thither, tossing, fading, leaping, but fading, always fading.

In a flash, like a printed picture on a screen, illuminated, keenly etched in the white glare, I see the bed, and the people around me, the black gowns, the pale eyes of the doctor, the sponge and basin, the rolls of lint.

Voices, minute but clean-cut and clear as picked harp-strings, tinkle in my ears; the voice of the doctor, other voices, but always the voice of the doctor—" The splinter of bone on the brain; the splinter pressing on the tissues; the depression."

The doctor! That is the man! That is the man who comes to my side, who follows, follows where I go, who seeks me throughout the world! I saw him as I lay flung on the turf, limp, unconscious, below the cliffs on the Aspen hills; I felt his presence in the studio; I heard him creeping at my heels across the gorse thickets of St. Gildas. And now he has come to cut short the magic second, to turn back time—back, back, into the old worn channels, rock-ribbed and salt with tears.

As a leaf of written paper torn in two, so shall my life be torn in two; and the long tear shall mangle the chapter written in rose and gold.

Then, too, my shadow, already turned from

white to gray, shall fall with a deeper stain wherever I pass; and I shall see the yellow gorse glimmer and turn to golden-rod, and the poplars turn to oaks; and the twin towers of Notre Dame, filmy, lace-carved, and gray with centuries, shall dwindle as I look—dwindle and sway and turn to pines, singing pines that murmur to the winds, blowing across the Aspen hills.

. . . .

All that is fair shall pass away; all that I love, all that I fear for—these shall the doctor take away, lifting them from my memory on the point of a steel blade. What has he to give in return? A hell of vapour, distorting sight; a hell of sound, drowning the soul.

. . . .

Gigantic apparitions arise across the world of water, wavering like shadows on the clouds. Steel-clad, clothed in skins, casqued in steel, their winged heads bend and nod and move against the clouds. And even they are changing as clouds change shape. I see steel limbs turn red and naked. I see winged casques trail to the earth, feathered, painted in colours of earth.

Ihó! Inâh! Etó! E-hó!

The bridge of stars spans the vast lake of air; the sun and the moon travel over it.

. . . .

My shadow is turning dark; I can scarcely

see the doctor, but now—God have mercy!—*I can touch him.*

. . . .

All the high spectres are stooping from the clouds, bending above me to watch. I know them and their eyes of shadow—I know them now; Hârpen that was to Chaskéwhat Hárpstinâ shall be to Hapéda; and Hârka shall come after all with the voice of winter winds:

" Aké u, aké u, aké u! "

But the magic second shall never return.

" Mâ cânté maséca! "

. . . .

Now they leave my bed, the people who crowded there under the shadowy forms of the spectres; now the doctor bends over; I see and feel him. His hands are tangled in the threads of time; he is cutting a thread; he——

XIX.

When I spoke to him first I spoke in the French language. Before he answered, the scream of a blue jay in the elms outside set my nerves aquiver, and I called for Donald and Walter.

As I lay there I could see the Aspen hills from the window, heaps of crumpled gold bathed in sunshine. Over them sailed the froth from the silken milkweed; over them drifted the big brown-red butterflies, luminous as richest autumn leaves.

Some one closed the door softly. The doctor had gone.

The sunlight poured into the window, etching my shadow on the wall behind. Lying very still there I saw it motionless beside me. *The shadow was black.*

Somebody said in the next room, " Will he die? "

" Die? " I said aloud.

A bird twittered outside my window.

The door opened again, noiselessly.

" Sweetheart? " I whispered.

" Yes, Jack."

After a moment I said, " When do you go back to school? "

" I? I finished school a year ago."

" Come nearer."

" I am here, Jack."

" Time stopped a year ago."

" A year ago to-day."

The same gray eyes, the same face, paler, perhaps.

" We have journeyed far," I sighed, " always together, but in those days our shadows were white as snow. Am I going to die? There are tears in your eyes."

They fell on my cheek; her arms fell too, closer, closer, around my neck.

" Life has begun," she said.

" Life? What was the year that ends to-day? The magic second of life? "

" A year of death, to me! "

Ah, but her soul knows of a life in death! And she shall know it, too, when her shadow turns whiter than snow. For the Temple of Idols has closed its doors at the sound of a voice, and an idol of gilt has turned to flesh and blood.

I-hó!

So shall she know of the life in death when her soul and her body are one.

PASSEUR.

O friends, I've served ye food and bed;
  O friends, the mist is rising wet;
Then bide a moment, O my dead,
  Where, lonely, I must linger yet!

176

PASSEUR.

Because man goeth to his long home,
And the mourners go about the streets.

WHEN he had finished his pipe he tapped
the brier bowl against the chimney until the
ashes powdered the charred log smouldering
across the andirons. Then he sank back in his
chair, absently touching the hot pipe-bowl with
the tip of each finger until it grew cool enough
to be dropped into his coat pocket.

Twice he raised his eyes to the little American clock ticking upon the mantel. He had
half an hour to wait.

The three candles that lighted the room
might be trimmed to advantage; this would
give him something to do. A pair of scissors
lay open upon the bureau, and he rose and
picked them up. For a while he stood dreamily
shutting and opening the scissors, his eyes roaming about the room. There was an easel in the
corner, and a pile of dusty canvases behind it;
behind the canvases there was a shadow—that
gray, menacing shadow that never moved.

When he had trimmed each candle he wiped

the smoky scissors on a paint rag and flung them on the bureau again. The clock pointed to ten; he had been occupied exactly three minutes.

The bureau was littered with neckties, pipes, combs and brushes, matches, reels and fly-books, collars, shirt studs, a new pair of Scotch shooting stockings, and a woman's workbasket.

He picked out all the neckties, folded them once, and hung them over a bit of twine that stretched across the looking-glass; the shirt studs he shovelled into the top drawer along with brushes, combs, and stockings; the reels and fly-books he dusted with his handkerchief and placed methodically along the mantel shelf. Twice he stretched out his hand toward the woman's workbasket, but his hand fell to his side again, and he turned away into the room staring at the dying fire.

Outside the snow-sealed window a shutter broke loose and banged monotonously, until he flung open the panes and fastened it. The soft, wet snow, that had choked the window-panes all day, was frozen hard now, and he had to break the polished crust before he could find the rusty shutter hinge.

He leaned out for a moment, his numbed hands resting on the snow, the roar of a rising snow-squall in his ears; and out across the desolate garden and stark hedgerow he saw the flat black river spreading through the gloom.

A candle sputtered and snapped behind him; a sheet of drawing-paper fluttered across the floor, and he closed the panes and turned back into the room, both hands in his worn pockets.

The little American clock on the mantel ticked and ticked, but the hands lagged, for he had not been occupied five minutes in all. He went up to the mantel and watched the hands of the clock. A minute—longer than a year to him—crept by.

Around the room the furniture stood ranged —a chair or two of yellow pine, a table, the easel, and in one corner the broad curtained bed; and behind each lay shadows, menacing shadows that never moved.

A little pale flame started up from the smoking log on the andirons; the room sang with the sudden hiss of escaping wood gases. After a little the back of the log caught fire; jets of blue flared up here and there with mellow sounds like the lighting of gas-burners in a row, and in a moment a thin sheet of yellow flame wrapped the whole charred log.

Then the shadows moved; not the shadows behind the furniture—they never moved—but other shadows, thin, gray, confusing, that came and spread their slim patterns all around him, and trembled and trembled.

He dared not step or tread upon them, they were too real; they meshed the floor around his feet, they ensnared his knees, they fell across his breast like ropes. Some night, in the silence of the moors, when wind and river were still, he feared these strands of shadow might tighten—creep higher around his throat and tighten. But even then he knew that those other shadows would never move, those gray shapes that knelt crouching in every corner.

When he looked up at the clock again ten minutes had straggled past. Time was disturbed in the room; the strands of shadow seemed entangled among the hands of the clock, dragging them back from their rotation. He wondered if the shadows would strangle Time, some still night when the wind and the flat river were silent.

There grew a sudden chill across the floor; the cracks of the boards let it in. He leaned down and drew his sabots toward him from their place near the andirons, and slipped them over his chaussons; and as he straightened up, his eyes mechanically sought the mantel above, where in the dusk another pair of sabots stood, little, slender, delicate sabots, carved from red beach. A year's dust grayed their surface; a year's rust dulled the silver band across the instep. He said this to himself aloud, knowing that it was within a few minutes of the year.

His own sabots came from Mort-Dieu; they were shaved square and banded with steel. But

in days past he had thought that no sabot in
Mort-Dieu was delicate enough to touch the
instep of the Mort-Dieu passeur. So he sent to
the shore lighthouse, and they sent to Lorient,
where the women are coquettish and show their
hair under the coiffe, and wear dainty sabots;
and in this town, where vanity corrupts and
their is much lace on coiffe and collarette, a pair
of delicate sabots was found, banded with silver
and chiselled in red beach. The sabots stood
on the mantel above the fire now, dusty and
tarnished.

There was a sound from the window, the soft
murmur of snow blotting glass panes. The
wind, too, muttered under the roof eaves. Presently it would begin to whisper to him from
the chimney—he knew it—and he held his
hands over his ears and stared at the clock.

In the hamlet of Mort-Dieu the pines sing
all day of the sea secrets, but in the night the
ghosts of little gray birds fill the branches,
singing of the sunshine of past years. He heard
the song as he sat, and he crushed his hands
over his ears; but the gray birds joined with
the wind in the chimney, and he heard all that
he dared not hear, and he thought all that he
dared not hope or think, and the swift tears
scalded his eyes.

In Mort-Dieu the nights are longer than
anywhere on earth; he knew it—why should he
not know? This had been so for a year; it

was different before. There were so many
things different before; days and nights vanished like minutes then; the pines told no secrets of the sea, and the gray birds had not yet
come to Mort-Dieu. Also, there was Jeanne,
passeur at the Carmes.

When he first saw her she was poling the
square, flat-bottomed ferry skiff from the Carmes
to Mort-Dieu, a red handkerchief bound across
her silky black hair, a red skirt fluttering just
below her knees. The next time he saw her he
had to call to her across the placid river, " Ohé!
Ohé, passeur! " She came, poling the flat skiff,
her deep blue eyes fixed pensively on him, the
scarlet skirt and kerchief idly flapping in the
April wind. Then day followed day when the
far call " Passeur! " grew clearer and more
joyous, and the faint answering cry, " I come! "
rippled across the water like music tinged with
laughter. Then spring came, and with spring
came love—love, carried free across the ferry
from the Carmes to Mort-Dieu.

The flame above the charred log whistled,
flickered, and went out in a jet of wood vapour,
only to play like lightning above the gas and
relight again. The clock ticked more loudly,
and the song from the pines filled the room.
But in his straining eyes a summer landscape
was reflected, where white clouds sailed and
white foam curled under the square bow of a
little skiff. And he pressed his numbed hands

tighter to his ears to drown the cry, "Passeur!
Passeur!"

And now for a moment the clock ceased
ticking. It was time to go—who but he should
know it, he who went out into the night swinging his lantern? And he went. He had gone
each night from the first—from that first
strange winter evening when a strange voice
had answered him across the river, the voice
of the new passeur. He had never heard *her*
voice again.

So he passed down the windy wooden stairs,
lantern hanging lighted in his hand, and
stepped out into the storm. Through sheets of
drifting snow, over heaps of frozen seaweed and
icy drift he moved, shifting his lantern right
and left, until its glimmer on the water warned
him. Then he called out into the night,
"Passeur!" The frozen spray spattered his
face and crusted the lantern; he heard the distant boom of breakers beyond the bar, and the
noise of mighty winds among the seaward cliffs.

"Passeur!"

Across the broad flat river, black as a sea of
pitch, a tiny light sparkled a moment. Again
he cried, "Passeur!"

"I come!"

He turned ghastly white, for it was her
voice—or was he crazy?—and he sprang waist
deep into the icy current and cried out again,
but his voice ended in a sob.

Slowly through the snow the flat skiff took shape, creeping nearer and nearer. But she was not at the pole—he saw that; there was only a tall, thin man, shrouded to the eyes in oilskin; and he leaped into the boat and bade the ferryman hasten.

Halfway across he rose in the skiff, and called, "Jeanne!" But the roar of the storm and the thrashing of icy waves drowned his voice. Yet he heard her again, and she called to him by name.

When at last the boat grated upon the invisible shore, he lifted his lantern, trembling, stumbling among the rocks, and calling to her, as though his voice could silence the voice that had spoken a year ago that night. And it could not. He sank shivering upon his knees, and looked out into the darkness, where an ocean rolled across a world. Then his stiff lips moved, and he repeated her name; but the hand of the ferryman fell gently upon his head.

And when he raised his eyes he saw that the ferryman was Death.

THE KEY TO GRIEF.

The moving finger writes, and, having writ,
   Moves on; nor all your piety nor wit
Shall lure it back to cancel half a line,
   Nor all your tears wash out a word of it.

THE KEY TO GRIEF.

The wild hawk to the wind-swept sky
    The deer to the wholesome wold,
And the heart of a man to the heart of a maid,
    As it was in the days of old.

KIPLING.

I.

THEY were doing their work very badly. They got the rope around his neck, and tied his wrists with moose-bush withes, but again he fell, sprawling, turning, twisting over the leaves, tearing up everything around him like a trapped panther.

He got the rope away from them; he clung to it with bleeding fists; he set his white teeth in it, until the jute strands relaxed, unravelled, and snapped, gnawed through by his white teeth.

Twice Tully struck him with a gum hook. The dull blows fell on flesh rigid as stone.

Panting, foul with forest mould and rotten leaves, hands and face smeared with blood, he sat up on the ground, glaring at the circle of men around him.

"Shoot him!" gasped Tully, dashing the

sweat from his bronzed brow; and Bates, breathing heavily, sat down on a log and dragged a revolver from his rear pocket. The man on the ground watched him; there was froth in the corners of his mouth.

" Git back! " whispered Bates, but his voice and hand trembled. " Kent," he stammered, " won't ye hang? "

The man on the ground glared.

" Ye've got to die, Kent," he urged; " they all say so. Ask Lefty Sawyer; ask Dyce; ask Carrots.—He's got to swing fur it—ain't he, Tully?—Kent, fur God's sake, swing fur these here gents! "

The man on the ground panted; his bright eyes never moved.

After a moment Tully sprang on him again. There was a flurry of leaves, a crackle, a gasp and a grunt, then the thumping and thrashing of two bodies writhing in the brush. Dyce and Carrots jumped on the prostrate men. Lefty Sawyer caught the rope again, but the jute strands gave way and he stumbled. Tully began to scream, " He's chokin' me! " Dyce staggered out into the open, moaning over a broken wrist.

" Shoot! " shouted Lefty Sawyer, and dragged Tully aside. " Shoot, Jim Bates! Shoot straight, b' God! "

" Git back! " gasped Bates, rising from the fallen log.

The crowd parted right and left; a quick report rang out—another—another. Then from the whirl of smoke a tall form staggered, dealing blows—blows that sounded sharp as the crack of a whip.

"He's off! Shoot straight!" they cried.

There was a gallop of heavy boots in the woods. Bates, faint and dazed, turned his head.

"Shoot!" shrieked Tully.

But Bates was sick; his smoking revolver fell to the ground; his white face and pale eyes contracted. It lasted only a moment; he started after the others, plunging, wallowing through thickets of osier and hemlock underbrush.

Far ahead he heard Kent crashing on like a young moose in November, and he knew he was making for the shore. The others knew too. Already the gray gleam of the sea cut a straight line along the forest edge; already the soft clash of the surf on the rocks broke faintly through the forest silence.

"He's got a canoe there!" bawled Tully. "He'll be into it!"

And he was into it, kneeling in the bow, driving his paddle to the handle. The rising sun gleamed like red lightning on the flashing blade; the canoe shot to the crest of a wave, hung, bows dripping in the wind, dropped into the depths, glided, tipped, rolled, shot up again, staggered, and plunged on.

Tully ran straight out into the cove surf; the water broke against his chest, bare and wet with sweat. Bates sat down on a worn black rock and watched the canoe listlessly.

The canoe dwindled to a speck of gray and silver; and when Carrots, who had run back to the gum camp for a rifle, returned, the speck on the water might have been easier to hit than a loon's head at twilight. So Carrots, being thrifty by nature, fired once, and was satisfied to save the other cartridges. The canoe was still visible, making for the open sea. Somewhere beyond the horizon lay the keys, a string of rocks bare as skulls, black and slimy where the sea cut their base, white on the crests with the excrement of sea birds.

" He's makin' fur the Key to Grief! " whispered Bates to Dyce.

Dyce, moaning, and nursing his broken wrist, turned a sick face out to sea.

The last rock seaward was the Key to Grief, a splintered pinnacle polished by the sea. From the Key to Grief, seaward a day's paddle, if a man dared, lay the long wooded island in the ocean known as Grief on the charts of the bleak coast.

In the history of the coast, two men had made the voyage to the Key to Grief, and from there to the island. One of these was a rum-crazed pelt hunter, who lived to come back; the other was a college youth; they found his battered canoe at sea, and a day later his battered body was flung up in the cove.

So, when Bates whispered to Dyce, and when Dyce called to the others, they knew that the end was not far off for Kent and his canoe; and they turned away into the forest, sullen, but satisfied that Kent would get his dues when the devil got his.

Lefty spoke vaguely of the wages of sin. Carrots, with an eye to thrift, suggested a plan for an equitable division of Kent's property.

When they reached the gum camp they piled Kent's personal effects on a blanket.

Carrots took the inventory: a revolver, two gum hooks, a fur cap, a nickel-plated watch, a pipe, a pack of new cards, a gum sack, forty pounds of spruce gum, and a frying pan.

Carrots shuffled the cards, picked out the joker, and flipped it pensively into the fire. Then he dealt cold decks all around.

When the goods and chattels of their late companion had been divided by chance—for there was no chance to cheat—somebody remembered Tully.

" He's down there on the coast, starin' after the canoe," said Bates huskily.

He rose and walked toward a heap on the ground covered by a blanket. He started to lift the blanket, hesitated, and finally turned away. Under the blanket lay Tully's brother, shot the night before by Kent.

"Guess we'd better wait till Tully comes," said Carrots uneasily. Bates and Kent had been campmates. An hour later Tully walked into camp.

He spoke to no one that day. In the morning Bates found him down on the coast digging, and said: "Hello, Tully! Guess we ain't much hell on lynchin'!"

"Naw," said Tully. "Git a spade."

"Goin' to plant him there?"

"Yep."

"Where he kin hear them waves?"

"Yep."

"Purty spot."

"Yep."

"Which way will he face?"

"Where he kin watch fur that damned canoe!" cried Tully fiercely.

"He—he can't see," ventured Bates uneasily. "He's dead, ain't he?"

"He'll heave up that there sand when the canoe comes back! An' it's a-comin'! An' Bud Kent'll be in it, dead or alive! Git a spade!"

The pale light of superstition flickered in Bates's eyes. He hesitated.

"The—the dead can't see," he began; "kin they?"

Tully turned a distorted face toward him.

"Yer lie!" he roared. "My brother kin see, dead or livin'! An' he'll see the hangin'

of Bud Kent! An' he'll git up outer the grave
fur to see it, Bill Bates! I'm tellin' ye! I'm
tellin' ye! Deep as I'll plant him, he'll heave
that there sand and call to me, when the canoe
comes in! I'll hear him; I'll be here! An'
we'll live to see the hangin' of Bud Kent! "

About sundown they planted Tully's
brother, face to the sea.

II.

On the Key to Grief the green waves rub
all day. White at the summit, black at the
base, the shafted rocks rear splintered pinna-
cles, slanting like channel buoys. On the polished pillars sea birds brood—white-winged,
bright-eyed sea birds, that nestle and preen
and flap and clatter their orange-coloured beaks
when the sifted spray drives and drifts across
the reef.

As the sun rose, painting crimson streaks
criss-cross over the waters, the sea birds sidled
together, huddling row on row, steeped in downy
drowse.

Where the sun of noon burnished the sea,
an opal wave washed, listless, noiseless; a sea
bird stretched one listless wing.

And into the silence of the waters a canoe
glided, bronzed by the sunlight, jewelled by the
salt drops stringing from prow to thwart, seaweed a-trail in the diamond-flashing wake, and
in the bow a man dripping with sweat.

Up rose the gulls, sweeping in circles, turning, turning over rock and sea, and their clamour filled the sky, starting little rippling echoes among the rocks.

The canoe grated on a shelf of ebony; the seaweed rocked and washed; the little sea crabs sheered sideways, down, down into limpid depths of greenest shadows. Such was the coming of Bud Kent to the Key to Grief.

He drew the canoe halfway up the shelf of rock and sat down, breathing heavily, one brown arm across the bow. For an hour he sat there. The sweat dried under his eyes. The sea birds came back, filling the air with soft querulous notes.

There was a livid mark around his neck, a red, raw circle. The salt wind stung it; the sun burned it into his flesh like a collar of red-hot steel. He touched it at times; once he washed it with cold salt water.

Far in the north a curtain of mist hung on the sea, dense, motionless as the fog on the Grand Banks. He never moved his eyes from it; he knew what it was. Behind it lay the Island of Grief.

All the year round the Island of Grief is hidden by the banks of mist, ramparts of dead white fog encircling it on every side. Ships give it wide berth. Some speak of warm springs on the island whose waters flow far out to sea, rising in steam eternally.

The pelt hunter had come back with tales of forests and deer and flowers everywhere; but he had been drinking much, and much was forgiven him.

The body of the college youth tossed up in the cove on the mainland was battered out of recognition, but some said, when found, one hand clutched a crimson blossom half wilted, but broad as a sap pan.

So Kent lay motionless beside his canoe, burned with thirst, every nerve vibrating, thinking of all these things. It was not fear that whitened the firm flesh under the tan; it was the fear of fear. He must not think—he must throttle dread; his eyes must never falter, his head never turn from that wall of mist across the sea. With set teeth he crushed back terror; with glittering eyes he looked into the hollow eyes of fright. And so he conquered fear.

He rose. The sea birds whirled up into the sky, pitching, tossing, screaming, till the sharp flapping of their pinions set the snapping echoes flying among the rocks.

Under the canoe's sharp prow the kelp bobbed and dipped and parted; the sunlit waves ran out ahead, glittering, dancing. Splash! splash! bow and stern! And now he knelt again, and the polished paddle swung and dipped, and swept and swung and dipped again.

Far behind, the clamour of the sea birds

lingered in his ears, till the mellow dip of the paddle drowned all sound and the sea was a sea of silence.

No wind came to cool the hot sweat on cheek and breast. The sun blazed a path of flame before him, and he followed out into the waste of waters. The still ocean divided under the bows and rippled innocently away on either side, tinkling, foaming, sparkling like the current in a woodland brook. He looked around at the world of flattened water, and the fear of fear rose up and gripped his throat again. Then he lowered his head, like a tortured bull, and shook the fear of fear from his throat, and drove the paddle into the sea as a butcher stabs, to the hilt.

So at last he came to the wall of mist. It was thin at first, thin and cool, but it thickened and grew warmer, and the fear of fear dragged at his head, but he would not look behind.

Into the fog the canoe shot; the gray water ran by, high as the gunwales, oily, silent. Shapes flickered across the bows, pillars of mist that rode the waters, robed in films of tattered shadows. Gigantic forms towered to dizzy heights above him, shaking out shredded shrouds of cloud. The vast draperies of the fog swayed and hung and trembled as he brushed them; the white twilight deepened to a sombre gloom. And now it grew thinner; the fog became a mist, and the mist a haze, and the haze floated away and vanished into the blue of the heavens.

All around lay a sea of pearl and sapphire, lapping, lapping on a silver shoal.

So he came to the Island of Grief.

III.

On the silver shoal the waves washed and washed, breaking like crushed opals where the sands sang with the humming froth.

Troops of little shore birds, wading on the shoal, tossed their sun-tipped wings and scuttled inland, where, dappled with shadow from the fringing forest, the white beach of the island stretched.

The water all around was shallow, limpid as crystal, and he saw the ribbed sand shining on the bottom, where purple seaweed floated, and delicate sea creatures darted and swarmed and scattered again at the dip of his paddle.

Like velvet rubbed on velvet the canoe brushed across the sand. He staggered to his feet, stumbled out, dragged the canoe high up under the trees, turned it bottom upward, and sank beside it, face downward in the sand. Sleep came to drive away the fear of fear, but hunger, thirst, and fever fought with sleep, and he dreamed—dreamed of a rope that sawed his neck, of the fight in the woods, and the shots. He dreamed, too, of the camp, of his forty pounds of spruce gum, of Tully, and of Bates. He dreamed of the fire and the smoke-scorched kettle, of the foul odour of musty bedding, of the greasy cards, and of his own new pack, hoarded for weeks to please the others. All this he dreamed, lying there face downward in the sand; but he did not dream of the face of the dead.

The shadows of the leaves moved on his blonde head, crisp with clipped curls. A butterfly flitted around him, alighting now on his legs, now on the back of his bronzed hands. All the afternoon the bees hung droning among the wildwood blossoms; the leaves above scarcely rustled; the shore birds brooded along the water's edge; the thin tide, sleeping on the sand, mirrored the sky.

Twilight paled the zenith; a breeze moved in the deeper woods; a star glimmered, went out, glimmered again, faded, and glimmered.

Night came. A moth darted to and fro under the trees; a beetle hummed around a heap of seaweed and fell scrambling in the sand. Somewhere among the trees a sound had become distinct, the song of a little brook, melodious, interminable. He heard it in his dream; it threaded all his dreams like a needle of silver, and like a needle it pricked him— pricked his dry throat and cracked lips. It could not awake him; the cool night swathed him head and foot.

Toward dawn a bird woke up and piped. Other birds stirred, restless, half awakened; a gull spread a cramped wing on the shore, preened its feathers, scratched its tufted neck, and took two drowsy steps toward the sea.

The sea breeze stirred out behind the mist bank; it raised the feathers on the sleeping gulls; it set the leaves whispering. A twig snapped, broke off, and fell. Kent stirred, sighed, trembled, and awoke.

The first thing he heard was the song of the brook, and he stumbled straight into the woods. There it lay, a thin, deep stream in the gray morning light, and he stretched himself beside it and laid his cheek in it. A bird drank in the pool, too—a little fluffy bird, bright-eyed and fearless.

His knees were firmer when at last he rose, heedless of the drops that beaded lips and chin. With his knife he dug and scraped at some white roots that hung half meshed in the bank of the brook, and when he had cleaned them in the pool he ate them.

The sun stained the sky when he went down to the canoe, but the eternal curtain of fog, far out at sea, hid it as yet from sight.

He lifted the canoe, bottom upwards, to his head, and, paddle and pole in either hand, carried it into the forest.

After he had set it down he stood a moment, opening and shutting his knife. Then he looked

up into the trees. There were birds there, if
he could get at them. He looked at the brook.
There were the prints of his fingers in the sand;
there, too, was the print of something else—a
deer's pointed hoof.

He had nothing but his knife. He opened
it again and looked at it.

That day he dug for clams and ate them
raw. He waded out into the shallows, too, and
jabbed at fish with his setting pole, but hit
nothing except a yellow crab.

Fire was what he wanted. He hacked and
chipped at flinty-looking pebbles, and scraped
tinder from a stick of sun-dried driftwood. His
knuckles bled, but no fire came.

That night he heard deer in the woods, and
could not sleep for thinking, until the dawn
came up behind the wall of mist, and he rose
with it to drink his fill at the brook and tear
raw clams with his white teeth. Again he
fought for fire, craving it as he had never
craved water, but his knuckles bled, and the
knife scraped on the flint in vain.

His mind, perhaps, had suffered somewhat.
The white beach seemed to rise and fall like a
white carpet on a gusty hearth. The birds,
too, that ran along the sand, seemed big and
juicy, like partridges; and he chased them,
hurling shells and bits of driftwood at them
till he could scarcely keep his feet for the rising, plunging beach—or carpet, whichever it

was. That night the deer aroused him at intervals. He heard them splashing and grunting and crackling along the brook. Once he arose and stole after them, knife in hand, till a false step into the brook awoke him to his folly, and he felt his way back to the canoe, trembling.

Morning came, and again he drank at the brook, lying on the sand where countless heart-shaped hoofs had passed leaving clean imprints; and again he ripped the raw clams from their shells and swallowed them, whimpering.

All day long the white beach rose and fell and heaved and flattened under his bright dry eyes. He chased the shore birds at times, till the unsteady beach tripped him up and he fell full length in the sand. Then he would rise moaning, and creep into the shadow of the wood, and watch the little song-birds in the branches, moaning, always moaning.

His hands, sticky with blood, hacked steel and flint together, but so feebly that now even the cold sparks no longer came.

He began to fear the advancing night; he dreaded to hear the big warm deer among the thickets. Fear clutched him suddenly, and he lowered his head and set his teeth and shook fear from his throat again.

Then he started aimlessly into the woods, crowding past bushes, scraping trees, treading on moss and twig and mouldy stump, his bruised hands swinging, always swinging.

The sun set in the mist as he came out of the woods on to another beach—a warm, soft beach, crimsoned by the glow in the evening clouds.

And on the sand at his feet lay a young girl asleep, swathed in the silken garment of her own black hair, round limbed, brown, smooth as the bloom on the tawny beach.

A gull flapped overhead, screaming. Her eyes, deeper than night, unclosed. Then her lips parted in a cry, soft with sleep, " Ihó! "

She rose, rubbing her velvet eyes. " Ihó! " she cried in wonder; " Inâh! "

The gilded sand settled around her little feet. Her cheeks crimsoned.

" E-hó! E-hó! " she whispered, and hid her face in her hair.

IV.

The bridge of the stars spans the sky seas; the sun and the moon are the travellers who pass over it. This was also known in the lodges of the Isantee, hundreds of years ago. Chaské told it to Hârpam, and when Hârpam knew he told it to Hapéda; and so the knowledge spread to Hârka, and from Winona to Wehârka, up and down, across and ever across, woof and web, until it came to the Island of Grief. And how? God knows!

Wehârka, prattling in the tules, may have told Ne-kâ; and Ne-kâ, high in the November

clouds, may have told Kay-óshk, who told it to
Shinge-bis, who told it to Skeé-skah, who told
it to Sé-só-Kah.

Ihó! Inâh! Behold the wonder of it! And
this is the fate of all knowledge that comes to
the Island of Grief.

.   .   .   .

As the red glow died in the sky, and the
sand swam in shadows, the girl parted the silken
curtains of her hair and looked at him.

" Ehó! " she whispered again in soft delight.

For now it was plain to her that he was the
sun! He had crossed the bridge of stars in the
blue twilight; he had come!

" E-tó! "

She stepped nearer, shivering, faint with
the ecstasy of this holy miracle wrought before her.

He was the Sun! His blood streaked the
sky at dawn; his blood stained the clouds at
even. In his eyes the blue of the sky still
lingered, smothering two blue stars; and his
body was as white as the breast of the Moon.

She opened both arms, hands timidly
stretched, palm upward. Her face was raised
to his, her eyes slowly closed; the deep-fringed
lids trembled.

Like a young priestess she stood, motionless
save for the sudden quiver of a limb, a quick
pulse-flutter in the rounded throat. And so
she worshipped, naked and unashamed, even

after he, reeling, fell heavily forward on his face; even when the evening breeze stealing over the sands stirred the hair on his head, as winds stir the fur of a dead animal in the dust.

. . . .

When the morning sun peered over the wall of mist, and she saw it was the sun, and she saw him, flung on the sand at her feet, then she knew that he was a man, only a man, pallid as death and smeared with blood.

And yet—miracle of miracles!—the divine wonder in her eyes deepened, and her body seemed to swoon, and fall a-trembling, and swoon again.

For, although it was but a man who lay at her feet, it had been easier for her to look upon a god.

He dreamed that he breathed fire—fire, that he craved as he had never craved water. Mad with delirium, he knelt before the flames, rubbing his torn hands, washing them in the crimson-scented flames. He had water, too, cool scented water, that sprayed his burning flesh, that washed in his eyes, his hair, his throat. After that came hunger, a fierce rending agony, that scorched and clutched and tore at his entrails; but that, too, died away, and he dreamed that he had eaten and all his flesh was warm. Then he dreamed that he slept; and when he slept he dreamed no more.

One day he awoke and found her stretched beside him, soft palms tightly closed, smiling, asleep.

v.

Now the days began to run more swiftly than the tide along the tawny beach; and the nights, star-dusted and blue, came and vanished and returned, only to exhale at dawn like perfume from a violet.

They counted hours as they counted the golden bubbles, winking with a million eyes along the foam-flecked shore; and the hours ended, and began, and glimmered, iridescent, and ended as bubbles end in a tiny rainbow haze.

There was still fire in the world; it flashed up at her touch and where she chose. A bow strung with the silk of her own hair, an arrow winged like a sea bird and tipped with shell, a line from the silver tendon of a deer, a hook of polished bone—these were the mysteries he learned, and learned them laughing, her silken head bent close to his.

The first night that the bow was wrought and the glossy string attuned, she stole into the moonlit forest to the brook; and there they stood, whispering, listening, and whispering, though neither understood the voice they loved.

In the deeper woods, Kaug, the porcupine, scraped and snuffed. They heard Wabóse, the rabbit, pit-a-pat, pit-a-pat, loping across dead leaves in the moonlight. Skeé-skah, the wood-duck, sailed past, noiseless, gorgeous as a floating blossom.

Out on the ocean's placid silver, Shinge-bis, the diver, shook the scented silence with his idle laughter, till Kay-óshk, the gray gull, stirred in his slumber. There came a sudden ripple in the stream, a mellow splash, a soft sound on the sand.

"Ihó! Behold!"

"I see nothing."

The beloved voice was only a wordless melody to her.

"Ihó! Ta-hinca, the red deer! E-hó! The buck will follow!"

"Ta-hinca," he repeated, notching the arrow.

"E-tó! Ta-mdóka!"

So he drew the arrow to the head, and the gray gull feathers brushed his ear, and the darkness hummed with the harmony of the singing string.

Thus died Ta-mdóka, the buck deer of seven prongs.

VI.

As an apple tossed spinning into the air, so spun the world above the hand that tossed it into space.

And one day in early spring, Sé-só-Kah, the

robin, awoke at dawn, and saw a girl at the foot
of the blossoming tree holding a babe cradled
in the silken sheets of her hair.

At its feeble cry, Kaug, the porcupine,
raised his quilled head. Wabóse, the rabbit,
sat still with palpitating sides. Kay-óshk, the
gray gull, tiptoed along the beach.

Kent knelt with one bronzed arm around
them both.

"Ihó! Inâh!" whispered the girl, and held
the babe up in the rosy flames of dawn.

But Kent trembled as he looked, and his
eyes filled. On the pale green moss their
shadows lay—three shadows. But the shadow
of the babe was white as froth.

Because it was the firstborn son, they named
it Chaské; and the girl sang as she cradled it
there in the silken vestments of her hair; all
day long in the sunshine she sang:

> Wâ-wa, wâ-wa, wâ-we—yeá;
> Kah-wéen, nee-zhéka Ke-diaus-âi,
> Ke-gâh nau-wâi, ne-mé-go S'weén,
> Ne-bâun, ne-bâun, ne-dâun-is âis.
> E-we wâ-wa, wâ-we—yeá;
> E-we wâ-wa, wâ-we—yeá.

Out in the calm ocean, Shinge-bis, the
diver, listened, preening his satin breast in silence. In the forest, Ta-hinca, the red deer,
turned her delicate head to the wind.

That night Kent thought of the dead, for

the first time since he had come to the Key of Grief.

"Aké-u! aké-u!" chirped Sé-só-Kah, the robin. But the dead never come again.

"Beloved, sit close to us," whispered the girl, watching his troubled eyes. "Ma-cânte maséca."

But he looked at the babe and its white shadow on the moss, and he only sighed: "Ma-cânte maséca, beloved! Death sits watching us across the sea."

Now for the first time he knew more than the fear of fear; he knew fear. And with fear came grief.

He never before knew that grief lay hidden there in the forest. Now he knew it. Still, that happiness, eternally reborn when two small hands reached up around his neck, when feeble fingers clutched his hand—that happiness that Sé-só-Kah understood, chirping to his brooding mate—that Ta-mdóka knew, licking his dappled fawns—that happiness gave him heart to meet grief calmly, in dreams or in the forest depths, and it helped him to look into the hollow eyes of fear.

He often thought of the camp now; of Bates, his blanket mate; of Dyce, whose wrist he had broken with a blow; of Tully, whose brother he had shot. He even seemed to hear the shot, the sudden report among the hemlocks; again he saw the haze of smoke, he caught a glimpse of a tall form falling through the bushes.

He remembered every minute incident of the trial: Bates's hand laid on his shoulder; Tully, red-bearded and wild-eyed, demanding his death; while Dyce spat and spat and smoked and kicked at the blackened log-ends projecting from the fire. He remembered, too, the verdict, and Tully's terrible laugh; and the new jute rope that they stripped off the market-sealed gum packs.

He thought of these things, sometimes wading out on the shoals, shell-tipped fish spear poised: at such times he would miss his fish. He thought of it sometimes when he knelt by the forest stream listening for Ta-hinca's splash among the cresses: at such moments the feathered shaft whistled far from the mark, and Ta-mdóka stamped and snorted till even the white fisher, stretched on a rotting log, flattened his whiskers and stole away into the forest's blackest depths.

When the child was a year old, hour for hour notched at sunset and sunrise, it prattled with the birds, and called to Ne-Kâ, the wild goose, who called again to the child from the sky: "Northward! northward, beloved!"

When winter came—there is no frost on the Island of Grief—Ne-Kâ, the wild goose, passing high in the clouds, called: "Southward! southward, beloved!" And the child answered in

a soft whisper of an unknown tongue, till the
mother shivered, and covered it with her silken
hair.

"O beloved!" said the girl, "Chaské calls
to all things living—to Kaug, the porcupine,
to Wabóse, to Kay-óshk, the gray gull—he calls,
and they understand."

Kent bent and looked into her eyes.

"Hush, beloved; it is not *that* I fear."

"Then what, beloved?"

"His shadow. It is white as surf foam.
And at night—I—I have seen——"

"Oh, what?"

"The air about him aglow like a pale rose."

"Ma cânté maséca. The earth alone lasts.
I speak as one dying—I know, O beloved!"

Her voice died away like a summer wind.

"Beloved!" he cried.

But there before him she was changing;
the air grew misty, and her hair wavered like
shreds of fog, and her slender form swayed, and
faded, and swerved, like the mist above a pond.

In her arms the babe was a figure of mist,
rosy, vague as a breath on a mirror.

"The earth alone lasts. Inâh! It is the
end, O beloved!"

The words came from the mist—a mist as
formless as the ether—a mist that drove in and
crowded him, that came from the sea, from
the clouds, from the earth at his feet. Faint
with terror, he staggered forward calling, "Be-

loved! And thou, Chaské, O beloved! Aké u!
Aké u!"

Far out at sea a rosy star glimmered an instant in the mist and went out.

A sea bird screamed, soaring over the waste
of fog-smothered waters. Again he saw the
rosy star; it came nearer; its reflection glimmered in the water.

"Chaské!" he cried.

He heard a voice, dull in the choking mist.

"O beloved, I am here!" he called again.

There was a sound on the shoal, a flicker in
the fog, the flare of a torch, a face white, livid,
terrible—the face of the dead.

He fell upon his knees; he closed his eyes
and opened them. Tully stood beside him with
a coil of rope.

.   .   .   .

Ihó! Behold the end! The earth alone
lasts. The sand, the opal wave on the golden
beach, the sea of sapphire, the dusted starlight,
the wind, and love, shall die. Death also shall
die, and lie on the shores of the skies like the
bleached skull there on the Key to Grief, polished, empty, with its teeth embedded in the
sand.

A MATTER OF INTEREST.

A MATTER OF INTEREST.

He that knows not, and knows not that he knows not, is
   a fool. Shun him.
He that knows not, and knows that he knows not, is
   simple. Teach him.
He that knows, and knows not that he knows, is asleep.
   Wake him.
He that knows, and knows that he knows, is wise.
   Follow him.   *Arabian Proverb.*

I.

MUCH as I dislike it, I am obliged to include
this story in a volume devoted to fiction: I have
attempted to tell it as an absolutely true story,
but until three months ago, when the indis-
putable proofs were placed before the British
Association by Professor James Holroyd, I was
regarded as an impostor. Now that the Smithsonian Institute in Washington, the Philadel-
phia Zoölogical Society, and the Natural History Museum of New York city, are convinced
that the story is truthful and accurate in every
particular, I prefer to tell it my own way. Professor Holroyd urges me to do this, although
Professor Bruce Stoddard, of Columbia College,

is now at work upon a pamphlet, to be published the latter part of next month, describing scientifically the extraordinary discovery which, to the shame of the United States, was first accepted and recognised in England.

Now, having no technical ability concerning the affair in question, and having no knowledge of either comparative anatomy or zoölogy, I am perhaps unfitted to tell this story. But the story is true; the episode occurred under my own eyes—here, within a few hours' sail of the Battery. And as I was one of the first persons to verify what has long been a theory among scientists, and, moreover, as the result of Professor Holroyd's discovery is to be placed on exhibition in Madison Square Garden on the twentieth of next month, I have decided to tell, as simply as I am able, exactly what occurred.

I first wrote out the story on April 1, 1896. The North American Review, the Popular Science Monthly, the Scientific American, Nature, Forest and Stream, and the Fossiliferous Magazine in turn rejected it; some curtly informing me that fiction had no place in their columns. When I attempted to explain that it was not fiction, the editors of these periodicals either maintained a contemptuous silence, or bluntly notified me that my literary services and opinions were not desired. But finally, when several publishers offered to take the story as fiction, I cut short all negotiations and decided to publish it myself. Where I am known at all, it is my misfortune to be known as a writer of fiction. This makes it impossible for me to receive a hearing from a scientific audience. I regret it bitterly, because now, when it is too late, I am prepared to prove certain scientific matters of interest, and to produce the proofs. In this case, however, I am fortunate, for nobody can dispute the existence of a thing when the bodily proof is exhibited as evidence.

This is the story; and if I write it as I write fiction, it is because I do not know how to write it otherwise.

I was walking along the beach below Pine Inlet, on the south shore of Long Island. The railroad and telegraph station is at West Oyster Bay. Everybody who has travelled on the Long Island Railroad knows the station, but few, perhaps, know Pine Inlet. Duck shooters, of course, are familiar with it; but as there are no hotels there, and nothing to see except salt meadow, salt creek, and a strip of dune and sand, the summer-squatting public may probably be unaware of its existence. The local name for the place is Pine Inlet; the maps give its name as Sand Point, I believe, but anybody at West Oyster Bay can direct you to it. Captain McPeek, who keeps the West Oyster Bay House, drives duck shooters there in winter. It lies five miles southeast from West Oyster Bay.

I had walked over that afternoon from Captain McPeek's. There was a reason for my going to Pine Inlet—it embarrasses me to explain it, but the truth is I meditated writing an ode to the ocean. It was out of the question to write it in West Oyster Bay, with the whistle of locomotives in my ears. I knew that Pine Inlet was one of the loneliest places on the Atlantic coast; it is out of sight of everything except leagues of gray ocean. Rarely one might make out fishing smacks drifting across the horizon. Summer squatters never visited it; sportsmen shunned it, except in winter. Therefore, as I was about to do a bit of poetry, I thought that Pine Inlet was the spot for the deed. So I went there.

As I was strolling along the beach, biting my pencil reflectively, tremendously impressed by the solitude and the solemn thunder of the surf, a thought occurred to me: how unpleasant it would be if I suddenly stumbled on a summer boarder. As this joyless impossibility flitted across my mind, I rounded a bleak sand dune.

A summer girl stood directly in my path.

If I jumped, I think the young lady has pardoned me by this time. She ought to, because she also started, and said something in a very faint voice. What she said was " Oh! "

She stared at me as though I had just crawled up out of the sea to bite her. I don't know what my own expression resembled, but I have been given to understand it was idiotic.

Now I perceived, after a few moments, that the young lady was frightened, and I knew I ought to say something civil. So I said, "Are there any mosquitoes here?"

"No," she replied, with a slight quiver in her voice; "I have only seen one, and it was biting somebody else."

I looked foolish; the conversation seemed so futile, and the young lady appeared to be more nervous than before. I had an impulse to say, "Do not run; I have breakfasted," for she seemed to be meditating a plunge into the breakers. What I did say was: "I did not know anybody was here. I do not intend to intrude. I come from Captain McPeek's, and I am writing an ode to the ocean." After I had said this it seemed to ring in my ears like, "I come from Table Mountain, and my name is Truthful James."

I glanced timidly at her.

"She's thinking of the same thing," said I to myself. "What an ass I must appear!"

However, the young lady seemed to be a trifle reassured. I noticed she drew a sigh of relief and looked at my shoes. She looked so long that it made me suspicious, and I also examined my shoes. They seemed to be fairly respectable.

"I—I am sorry," she said, "but would you mind not walking on the beach?"

This was sudden. I had intended to retire and leave the beach to her, but I did not fancy being driven away so abruptly.

"I was about to withdraw, madam," said I, bowing stiffly; "I beg you will pardon any inconvenience——"

"Dear me!" she cried, "you don't understand. I do not—I would not think for a moment of asking you to leave Pine Inlet. I merely ventured to request you to walk on the dunes. I am so afraid that your footprints may obliterate the impressions that my father is studying."

"Oh!" said I, looking about me as though I had been caught in the middle of a flower-bed; "really I did not notice any impressions. Impressions of what—if I may be permitted?"

"I don't know," she said, smiling a little at my awkward pose. "If you step this way in a straight line you can do no damage."

I did as she bade me. I suppose my movements resembled the gait of a wet peacock. Possibly they recalled the delicate manœuvres of the kangaroo. Anyway, she laughed.

This seriously annoyed me. I had been at a disadvantage; I walk well enough when let alone.

"You can scarcely expect," said I, "that a man absorbed in his own ideas could notice im-

pressions on the sand. I trust I have obliter-
ated nothing."

As I said this I looked back at the long line
of footprints stretching away in prospective
across the sand. They were my own. How
large they looked! Was that what she was
laughing at?

" I wish to explain," she said gravely, looking at the point of her parasol. " I am very
sorry to be obliged to warn you—to ask you to
forego the pleasure of strolling on a beach that
does not belong to me. Perhaps," she continued, in sudden alarm, " perhaps this beach be-
longs to you? "

" The beach? Oh, no," I said.

" But—but you were going to write poems
about it? "

" Only one—and that does not necessitate
owning the beach. I have observed," said I
frankly, " that the people who own nothing
write many poems about it."

She looked at me seriously.

" I write many poems," I added.

She laughed doubtfully.

" Would you rather I went away? " I asked
politely.

" I? Why, no—I mean that you may do
as you please—except please do not walk on the
beach."

" Then I do not alarm you by my presence? " I inquired. My clothes were a bit

ancient. I wore them shooting, sometimes. "My family is respectable," I added; and I told her my name.

"Oh! Then you wrote 'Culled Cowslips' and 'Faded Fig-Leaves,' and you imitate Maeterlinck, and you—— Oh, I know lots of people that you know;" she cried with every symptom of relief; "and you know my brother."

"I am the author," said I coldly, "of 'Culled Cowslips,' but 'Faded Fig-Leaves' was an earlier work, which I no longer recognise, and I should be grateful to you if you would be kind enough to deny that I ever imitated Maeterlinck. Possibly," I added, "he imitates me."

"Now, do you know," she said, "I was afraid of you at first? Papa is digging in the salt meadows nearly a mile away."

It was hard to bear.

"Can you not see," said I, "that I am wearing a shooting coat?"

"I do see—now; but it is so—so old," she pleaded.

"It is a shooting coat all the same," I said bitterly.

She was very quiet, and I saw she was sorry.

"Never mind," I said magnanimously, "you probably are not familiar with sporting goods. If I knew your name I should ask permission to present myself."

"Why, I am Daisy Holroyd," she said.

"What! Jack Holroyd's little sister?"

"Little!" she cried.

"I didn't mean that," said I. "You know that your brother and I were great friends in Paris——"

"I know," she said significantly.

"Ahem! Of course," I said, "Jack and I were inseparable——"

"Except when shut in separate cells," said Miss Holroyd coldly.

This unfeeling allusion to the unfortunate termination of a Latin-Quarter celebration hurt me.

"The police," said I, "were too officious."

"So Jack says," replied Miss Holroyd demurely.

We had unconsciously moved on along the sand hills, side by side, as we spoke.

"To think," I repeated, "that I should meet Jack's little——"

"Please," she said, "you are only three years my senior."

She opened the sunshade and tipped it over one shoulder. It was white, and had spots and posies on it.

"Jack sends us every new book you write," she observed. "I do not approve of some things you write."

"Modern school," I mumbled.

"That is no excuse," she said severely; "Anthony Trollope didn't do it."

The foam spume from the breakers was drifting across the dunes, and the little tip-up snipe ran along the beach and teetered and whistled and spread their white-barred wings for a low, straight flight across the shingle, only to tip and skeep and sail on again. The salt sea wind whistled and curled through the crested waves, blowing in perfumed puffs across thickets of sweet bay and cedar. As we passed through the crackling juicy-stemmed marsh weed myriads of fiddler crabs raised their fore-claws in warning and backed away, rustling, through the reeds, aggressive, protesting.

"Like millions of pigmy Ajaxes defying the lightning," I said.

Miss Holroyd laughed.

"Now I never imagined that authors were clever except in print," she said.

She was a most extraordinary girl.

"I suppose," she observed after a moment's silence—"I suppose I am taking you to my father."

"Delighted!" I mumbled. "H'm! I had the honour of meeting Professor Holroyd in Paris."

"Yes; he bailed you and Jack out," said Miss Holroyd serenely.

The silence was too painful to last.

"Captain McPeek is an interesting man," I said. I spoke more loudly than I intended; I may have been nervous.

"Yes," said Daisy Holroyd, "but he has a most singular hotel clerk."

"You mean Mr. Frisby?"

"I do."

"Yes," I admitted, "Mr. Frisby is queer. He was once a bill-poster."

"I know it!" exclaimed Daisy Holroyd, with some heat. "He ruins landscapes whenever he has an opportunity. Do you know that he has a passion for bill-posting? He has; he posts bills for the pure pleasure of it, just as you play golf, or tennis, or billiards."

"But he's a hotel clerk now," I said; "nobody employs him to post bills."

"I know it! He does it all by himself for the pure pleasure of it. Papa has engaged him to come down here for two weeks, and I dread it," said the girl.

What Professor Holroyd might want of Frisby I had not the faintest notion. I suppose Miss Holroyd noticed the bewilderment in my face, for she laughed, and nodded her head twice.

"Not only Mr. Frisby, but Captain McPeek also," she said.

"You don't mean to say that Captain McPeek is going to close his hotel!" I exclaimed.

My trunk was there. It contained guarantees of my respectability.

"Oh, no; his wife will keep it open," replied the girl. "Look! you can see papa now. He's digging."

"Where?" I blurted out.

I remembered Professor Holroyd as a prim, spectacled gentleman, with close-cut, snowy beard and a clerical allure. The man I saw digging wore green goggles, a jersey, a battered sou'wester, and hip-boots of rubber. He was delving in the muck of the salt meadow, his face streaming with perspiration, his boots and jersey splashed with unpleasant-looking mud. He glanced up as we approached, shading his eyes with a sunburnt hand.

"Papa, dear," said Miss Holroyd, "here is Jack's friend, whom you bailed out of Mazas."

The introduction was startling. I turned crimson with mortification. The professor was very decent about it; he called me by name at once.

When he said this he looked at his spade. It was clear that he considered me a nuisance and wished to go on with his digging.

"I suppose," he said, "you are still writing?"

"A little," I replied, trying not to speak sarcastically. My output had rivaled that of "The Duchess"—in quantity, I mean.

"I seldom read—fiction," he said, looking restlessly at the hole in the ground.

Miss Holroyd came to my rescue.

"That was a charming story you wrote last," she said. "Papa should read it—you should, papa; it's all about a fossil."

We both looked narrowly at Miss Holroyd. Her smile was guileless.

"Fossils!" repeated the professor. "Do you care for fossils?"

"Very much," said I.

Now I am not perfectly sure what my object was in lying. I looked at Daisy Holroyd's dark-fringed eyes. They were very grave.

"Fossils," said I, "are my hobby."

I think Miss Holroyd winced a little at this. I did not care. I went on:

"I have seldom had the opportunity to study the subject, but, as a boy, I collected flint arrow-heads——"

"Flint arrow-heads!" said the professor coldly.

"Yes; they were the nearest things to fossils obtainable," I replied, marvelling at my own mendacity.

The professor looked into the hole. I also looked. I could see nothing in it. "He's digging for fossils," thought I to myself.

"Perhaps," said the professor cautiously, "you might wish to aid me in a little research— that is to say, if you have an inclination for fossils." The double-entendre was not lost upon me.

"I have read all your books so eagerly,"

said I, "that to join you, to be of service to you in any research, however difficult and trying, would be an honour and a privilege that I never dared to hope for."

"That," thought I to myself, "will do its own work."

But the professor was still suspicious. How could he help it, when he remembered Jack's escapades, in which my name was always blended! Doubtless he was satisfied that my influence on Jack was evil. The contrary was the case, too.

"Fossils," he said, worrying the edges of the excavation with his spade, "fossils are not things to be lightly considered."

"No, indeed!" I protested.

"Fossils are the most interesting as well as puzzling things in the world," said he.

"They are!" I cried enthusiastically.

"But I am not looking for fossils," observed the professor mildly.

This was a facer. I looked at Daisy Holroyd. She bit her lip and fixed her eyes on the sea. Her eyes were wonderful eyes.

"Did you think I was digging for fossils in a salt meadow?" queried the professor. "You can have read very little about the subject. I am digging for something quite different."

I was silent. I knew that my face was a trifle flushed. I longed to say, "Well, what the devil are you digging for?" but I only stared into the hole as though hypnotized.

"Captain McPeek and Frisby ought to be here," he said, looking first at Daisy and then across the meadows.

I ached to ask him why he had subpœnaed Captain McPeek and Frisby.

"They are coming," said Daisy, shading her eyes. "Do you see the speck on the meadows?"

"It may be a mud hen," said the professor.

"Miss Holroyd is right," I said. "A wagon and team and two men are coming from the north. There is a dog beside the wagon— it's that miserable yellow dog of Frisby's."

"Good gracious!" cried the professor, "you don't mean to tell me that you see all that at such a distance?"

"Why not?" I said.

"I see nothing," he insisted.

"You will see that I'm right, presently," I laughed.

The professor removed his blue goggles and rubbed them, glancing obliquely at me.

"Haven't you heard what extraordinary eyesight duck shooters have?" said his daughter, looking back at her father. "Jack says that they can tell exactly what kind of a duck is flying before most people could see anything at all in the sky."

"It's true," I said; "it comes to anybody, I fancy, who has had practice."

The professor regarded me with a new interest. There was inspiration in his eyes. He turned toward the ocean. For a long time he stared at the tossing waves on the beach, then he looked far out to where the horizon met the sea.

"Are there any ducks out there?" he asked at last.

"Yes," said I, scanning the sea, "there are."

He produced a pair of binoculars from his coat-tail pocket, adjusted them, and raised them to his eyes.

"H'm! What sort of ducks?"

I looked more carefully, holding both hands over my forehead.

"Surf ducks—scoters and widgeon. There is one bufflehead among them—no, two; the rest are coots," I replied.

"This," cried the professor, "is most astonishing. I have good eyes, but I can't see a blessed thing without these binoculars!"

"It's not extraordinary," said I; "the surf ducks and coots any novice might recognise; the widgeon and buffleheads I should not have been able to name unless they had risen from the water. It is easy to tell any duck when it is flying, even though it looks no bigger than a black pin-point."

But the professor insisted that it was marvellous, and he said that I might render him invaluable service if I would consent to come and camp at Pine Inlet for a few weeks.

I looked at his daughter, but she turned her back—not exactly in disdain either. Her back was beautifully moulded. Her gown fitted also.

Camp out here?" I repeated, pretending to be unpleasantly surprised.

"I do not think he would care to," said Miss Holroyd without turning.

I had not expected that.

"Above all things," said I, in a clear, pleasant voice, "I like to camp out."

She said nothing.

"It is not exactly camping," said the professor. "Come, you shall see our conservatory. Daisy, come, dear! you must put on a heavier frock; it is getting toward sundown."

At that moment, over a near dune, two horses' heads appeared, followed by two human heads, then a wagon, then a yellow dog.

I turned triumphantly to the professor.

"You are the very man I want," he muttered; "the very man—the very man."

I looked at Daisy Holroyd. She returned my glance with a defiant little smile.

"Waal," said Captain McPeek, driving up, "here we be! Git out, Frisby."

Frisby, fat, nervous, and sentimental, hopped out of the cart.

"Come!" said the professor, impatiently moving across the dunes. I walked with Daisy Holroyd. McPeek and Frisby followed. The yellow dog walked by himself.

II.

The sun was dipping into the sea as we trudged across the meadows toward a high dome-shaped dune covered with cedars and thickets of sweet bay. I saw no sign of habitation among the sand hills. Far as the eye could reach, nothing broke the gray line of sea and sky save the squat dunes crowned with stunted cedars.

Then, as we rounded the base of the dune, we almost walked into the door of a house. My amazement amused Miss Holroyd, and I noticed also a touch of malice in her pretty eyes. But she said nothing, following her father into the house, with the slightest possible gesture to me. Was it invitation, or was it menace?

The house was merely a light wooden frame, covered with some waterproof stuff that looked like a mixture of rubber and tar. Over this— in fact, over the whole roof—was pitched an awning of heavy sail-cloth. I noticed that the house was anchored to the sand by chains, already rusted red. But this one-storied house was not the only building nestling in the south shelter of the big dune. A hundred feet away stood another structure—long, low, also built of wood. It had rows on rows of round port-holes on every side. The ports were fitted with heavy glass, hinged to swing open if neces-sary. A single big double door occupied the front.

Behind this long, low building was still another, a mere shed. Smoke rose from the sheet-iron chimney. There was somebody mov-ing about inside the open door.

As I stood gaping at this mushroom hamlet the professor appeared at the door and asked me to enter. I stepped in at once.

The house was much larger than I had im-agined. A straight hallway ran through the centre from east to west. On either side of this hallway were rooms, the doors swinging wide open. I counted three doors on each side; the three on the south appeared to be bedrooms.

The professor ushered me into a room on the north side, where I found Captain McPeek and Frisby sitting at a table, upon which were drawings and sketches of articulated animals and fishes.

" You see, McPeek," said the professor, " we only wanted one more man, and I think I've got him.—Haven't I? " turning eagerly to me.

"Why, yes," I said, laughing; "this is delightful. Am I invited to stay here?"

"Your bedroom is the third on the south side; everything is ready. McPeek, you can bring his trunk to-morrow, can't you?" demanded the professor.

The red-faced captain nodded, and shifted a quid.

"Then it's all settled," said the professor, and he drew a sigh of satisfaction. "You see," he said, turning to me, "I was at my wit's end to know whom to trust. I never thought of you. Jack's out in China, and I didn't dare trust anybody in my own profession. All you care about is writing verses and stories, isn't it?"

"I like to shoot," I replied mildly.

"Just the thing!" he cried, beaming at us all in turn. "Now I can see no reason why we should not progress rapidly. McPeek, you and Frisby must get those boxes up here before dark. Dinner will be ready before you have finished unloading. Dick, you will wish to go to your room first."

My name isn't Dick, but he spoke so kindly, and beamed upon me in such a fatherly manner, that I let it go. I had occasion to correct him afterward, several times, but he always forgot the next minute. He calls me Dick to this day.

It was dark when Professor Holroyd, his

daughter, and I sat down to dinner. The room was the same in which I had noticed the drawings of beast and bird, but the round table had been extended into an oval, and neatly spread with dainty linen and silver.

A fresh-cheeked Swedish girl appeared from a further room, bearing the soup. The professor ladled it out, still beaming.

"Now, this is very delightful!—isn't it, Daisy?" he said.

"Very," said Miss Holroyd, with the faintest tinge of irony.

"Very," I repeated heartily; but I looked at my soup when I said it.

"I suppose," said the professor, nodding mysteriously at his daughter, "that Dick knows nothing of what we're about down here?"

"I suppose," said Miss Holroyd, "that he thinks we are digging for fossils."

I looked at my plate. She might have spared me that.

"Well, well," said her father, smiling to himself, "he shall know everything by morning. You'll be astonished, Dick, my boy."

"His name isn't Dick," corrected Daisy.

The professor said, "Isn't it?" in an absent-minded way, and relapsed into contemplation of my necktie.

I asked Miss Holroyd a few questions about Jack, and was informed that he had given up law and entered the diplomatic service—as what, I did not dare ask, for I know what our diplomatic service is.

"In China," said Daisy.

"Choo Choo is the name of the city," added her father proudly; "it's the terminus of the new trans-Siberian railway."

"It's on the Yellow River," said Daisy.

"He's vice-consul," added the professor triumphantly.

"He'll make a good one," I observed. I knew Jack. I pitied his consul.

So we chatted on about my old playmate, until Freda, the red-cheeked maid, brought coffee, and the professor lighted a cigar, with a little bow to his daughter.

"Of course, you don't smoke," she said to me, with a glimmer of malice in her eyes.

"He mustn't," interposed the professor hastily; "it will make his hand tremble."

"No, it doesn't," said I, laughing; "but my hand will shake if I don't smoke. Are you going to employ me as a draughtsman?"

"You'll know to-morrow," he chuckled, with a mysterious smile at his daughter.— "Daisy, give him my best cigars; put the box here on the table. We can't afford to have his hand tremble."

Miss Holroyd rose, and crossed the hallway to her father's room, returning presently with a box of promising-looking cigars.

"I don't think he knows what is good for

him," she said. "He should smoke only one every day."

It was hard to bear. I am not vindictive, but I decided to treasure up a few of Miss Holroyd's gentle taunts. My intimacy with her brother was certainly a disadvantage to me now. Jack had apparently been talking too much, and his sister appeared to be thoroughly acquainted with my past. It was a disadvantage. I remembered her vaguely as a girl with long braids, who used to come on Sundays with her father and take tea with us in our rooms. Then she went to Germany to school, and Jack and I employed our Sunday evenings otherwise. It is true that I regarded her weekly visits as a species of infliction, but I did not think I ever showed it.

"It is strange," said I, "that you did not recognise me at once, Miss Holroyd. Have I changed so greatly in five years?"

"You wore a pointed French beard in Paris," she said—"a very downy one. And you never stayed to tea but twice, and then you only spoke once."

"Oh!" said I blankly. "What did I say?"

"You asked me if I liked plums," said Daisy, bursting into an irresistible ripple of laughter.

I saw that I must have made the same sort of an ass of myself that most boys of eighteen do.

It was too bad. I never thought about the future in those days. Who could have imagined that little Daisy Holroyd would have grown up into this bewildering young lady? It was really too bad. Presently the professor retired to his room, carrying with him an armful of drawings, and bidding us not to sit up late. When he closed his door Miss Holroyd turned to me.

" Papa will work over those drawings until midnight," she said, with a despairing smile.

" It isn't good for him," I said. " What are the drawings? "

" You may know to-morrow," she answered, leaning forward on the table and shading her face with one hand. " Tell me about yourself and Jack in Paris."

I looked at her suspiciously.

" What!   There isn't much to tell. We studied. Jack went to the law school, and I attended—er—oh, all sorts of schools."

" Did you?   Surely you gave yourself a little recreation occasionally? "

" Occasionally," I nodded.

" I am afraid you and Jack studied too hard."

" That may be," said I, looking meek.

" Especially about fossils."

I couldn't stand that.

" Miss Holroyd," I said, " I do care for fossils. You may think that I am a humbug, but I have a perfect mania for fossils—now."

"Since when?"

"About an hour ago," I said airily. Out of the corner of my eye I saw that she had flushed up. It pleased me.

"You will soon tire of the experiment," she said with a dangerous smile.

"Oh, I may," I replied indifferently.

She drew back. The movement was scarcely perceptible, but I noticed it, and she knew I did.

The atmosphere was vaguely hostile. One feels such mental conditions and changes instantly. I picked up a chessboard, opened it, set up the pieces with elaborate care, and began to move, first the white, then the black. Miss Holroyd watched me coldly at first, but after a dozen moves she became interested and leaned a shade nearer. I moved a black pawn forward.

"Why do you do that?" said Daisy.

"Because," said I, "the white queen threatens the pawn."

"It was an aggressive move," she insisted.

"Purely defensive," I said. "If her white highness will let the pawn alone, the pawn will let the queen alone."

Miss Holroyd rested her chin on her wrist and gazed steadily at the board. She was flushing furiously, but she held her ground.

"If the white queen doesn't block that pawn, the pawn may become dangerous," she said coldly.

I laughed, and closed up the board with a snap.

"True," I said, "it might even take the queen." After a moment's silence I asked, "What would you do in that case, Miss Holroyd?"

"I should resign," she said serenely; then realizing what she had said, she lost her self-possession for a second, and cried: "No, indeed! I should fight to the bitter end! I mean——"

"What?" I asked, lingering over my revenge.

"I mean," she said slowly, "that your black pawn would never have the chance—never! I should take it immediately."

"I believe you would," said I, smiling; "so we'll call the game yours, and—the pawn captured."

"I don't want it," she exclaimed. "A pawn is worthless."

"Except when it's in the king row."

"Chess is most interesting," she observed sedately. She had completely recovered her self-control. Still I saw that she now had a certain respect for my defensive powers. It was very soothing to me.

"You know," said I gravely, "that I am

fonder of Jack than of anybody. That's the reason we never write each other, except to borrow things. I am afraid that when I was a young cub in France I was not an attractive personality."

"On the contrary," said Daisy, smiling, "I thought you were very big and very perfect. I had illusions. I wept often when I went home and remembered that you never took the trouble to speak to me but once."

"I was a cub," I said; "not selfish and brutal, but I didn't understand schoolgirls. I never had any sisters, and I didn't know what to say to very young girls. If I had imagined that you felt hurt——"

"Oh, I did—five years ago. Afterward I laughed at the whole thing."

"Laughed?" I repeated, vaguely disappointed.

"Why, of course. I was very easily hurt when I was a child. I think I have outgrown it."

The soft curve of her sensitive mouth contradicted her.

"Will you forgive me now?" I asked.

"Yes. I had forgotten the whole thing until I met you an hour or so ago."

There was something that had a ring not entirely genuine in this speech. I noticed it, but forgot it the next moment.

"Tiger cubs have stripes," said I. "Selfishness blossoms in the cradle, and prophecy is not difficult. I hope I am not more selfish than my brothers."

"I hope not," she said, smiling.

Presently she rose, touched her hair with the tip of one finger, and walked to the door.

"Good-night," she said, courtesying very low.

"Good-night," said I, opening the door for her to pass.

III.

The sea was a sheet of silver, tinged with pink. The tremendous arch of the sky was all shimmering and glimmering with the promise of the sun. Already the mist above, flecked with clustered clouds, flushed with rose colour and dull gold. I heard the low splash of the waves breaking and curling across the beach. A wandering breeze, fresh and fragrant, blew the curtains of my window. There was the scent of sweet bay in the room, and everywhere the subtile, nameless perfume of the sea.

When at last I stood upon the shore, the air and sea were all aglimmer in a rosy light, deepening to crimson in the zenith. Along the beach I saw a little cove, shelving and all ashine, where shallow waves washed with a mellow sound. Fine as dusted gold the shingle glowed, and the thin film of water rose, receded, crept up again a little higher, and again flowed

back, with the low hiss of snowy foam and
gilded bubbles breaking.

I stood a little while quiet, my eyes upon
the water, the invitation of the ocean in my
ears, vague and sweet as the murmur of a shell.
Then I looked at my bathing suit and towels.

"In we go!" said I aloud.   A second later
the prophecy was fulfilled.

I swam far out to sea, and as I swam the
waters all around me turned to gold.   The sun
had risen.

There is a fragrance in the sea at dawn that
none can name.   Whitethorn abloom in May,
sedges asway, and scented rushes rustling in
an inland wind recall the sea to me—I can't say
why.

Far out at sea I raised myself, swung
around, dived, and set out again for shore, strik-
ing strong strokes until the flecked foam flew.
And when at last I shot through the breakers,
I laughed aloud and sprang upon the beach,
breathless and happy.   Then from the ocean
came another cry, clear, joyous, and a white
arm rose in the air.

She came drifting in with the waves like
a white sea-sprite, laughing at me from her
tangled hair, and I plunged into the breakers
again to join her.

Side by side we swam along the coast, just
outside the breakers, until in the next cove we
saw the flutter of her maid's cap strings.

"I will beat you to breakfast!" she cried, as I rested, watching her glide up along the beach.

"Done!" said I—"for a sea-shell!"

"Done!" she called across the water.

I made good speed along the shore, and I was not long in dressing, but when I entered the dining-room she was there, demure, smiling, exquisite in her cool, white frock.

"The sea-shell is yours," said I. "I hope I can find one with a pearl in it."

The professor hurried in before she could reply. He greeted me very cordially, but there was an abstracted air about him, and he called me Dick until I recognised that remonstrance was useless. He was not long over his coffee and rolls.

"McPeek and Frisby will return with the last load, including your trunk, by early afternoon," he said, rising and picking up his bundle of drawings. "I haven't time to explain to you what we are doing, Dick, but Daisy will take you about and instruct you. She will give you the rifle standing in my room—it's a good Winchester. I have sent for an 'Express' for you, big enough to knock over any elephant in India.—Daisy, take him through the sheds and tell him everything. Luncheon is at noon. —Do you usually take luncheon, Dick?"

"When I am permitted," I smiled.

"Well," said the professor doubtfully, "you mustn't come back here for it. Freda can take

you what you want. Is your hand unsteady
after eating? "

"Why, papa! " said Daisy. " Do you intend to starve him? "

We all laughed.

The professor tucked his drawings into a
capacious pocket, pulled his sea boots up to his
hips, seized a spade, and left, nodding to us
as though he were thinking of something else.

We went to the door and watched him across
the salt meadows until a distant sand dune hid
him.

" Come," said Daisy Holroyd, "I am going
to take you to the shop."

She put on a broad-brimmed straw hat, a
distractingly pretty combination of filmy cool
stuffs, and led the way to the long low structure that I had noticed the evening before.

The interior was lighted by the numberless
little portholes, and I could see everything
plainly. I acknowledge I was nonplussed by
what I did see.

In the centre of the shed, which must have
been at least a hundred feet long, stood what
I thought at first was the skeleton of an enormous whale. After a moment's silent contemplation of the thing I saw that it could not be
a whale, for the frames of two gigantic bat-like
wings rose from each shoulder. Also I noticed
that the animal possessed legs—four of them—
with most unpleasant-looking webbed claws

fully eight feet long. The bony framework of the head, too, resembled something between a crocodile and a monstrous snapping turtle. The walls of the shanty were hung with drawings and blue prints. A man dressed in white linen was tinkering with the vertebræ of the lizard-like tail.

"Where on earth did such a reptile come from?" I asked at length.

"Oh, it's not real!" said Daisy scornfully; "it's papier-maché."

"I see," said I—"a stage prop."

"A what?" asked Daisy, in hurt astonishment.

"Why, a—a sort of Siegfried dragon—a what's-his-name—er, Pfafner, or Peffer, or——"

"If my father heard you say such things he would dislike you," said Daisy. She looked grieved, and moved toward the door. I apologized—for what, I knew not—and we became reconciled. She ran into her father's room and brought me the rifle, a very good Winchester. She also gave me a cartridge belt, full.

"Now," she smiled, "I shall take you to your observatory, and when we arrive you are to begin your duty at once."

"And that duty?" I ventured, shouldering the rifle.

"That duty is, to watch the ocean. I shall then explain the whole affair—but you mustn't look at me while I speak; you must watch the sea."

"This," said I, " is hardship. I had rather go without the luncheon."

I do not think she was offended at my speech; still she frowned for almost three seconds.

We passed through acres of sweet bay and spear grass, sometimes skirting thickets of twisted cedars, sometimes walking in the full glare of the morning sun, sinking into shifting sand where sun-scorched shells crackled under our feet, and sun-browned seaweed glistened, bronzed and iridescent. Then, as we climbed a little hill, the sea wind freshened in our faces, and lo! the ocean lay below us, far-stretching as the eye could reach, glittering, magnificent.

Daisy sat down flat on the sand. It takes a clever girl to do that and retain the respectful deference due her from men. It takes a graceful girl to accomplish it triumphantly when a man is looking.

"You must sit beside me," she said—as though it would prove irksome to me.

"Now," she continued, "you must watch the water while I am talking."

I nodded.

"Why don't you do it, then?" she asked.

I succeeded in wrenching my head toward the ocean, although I felt sure it would swing gradually round again in spite of me.

"To begin with," said Daisy Holroyd, "there's a thing in that ocean that would astonish you if you saw it. Turn your head!"

"I am," I said meekly.

"Did you hear what I said?"

"Yes—er—a thing in the ocean that's going to astonish me." Visions of mermaids rose before me.

"The thing," said Daisy, "is a Thermosaurus!"

I nodded vaguely, as though anticipating a delightful introduction to a nautical friend.

"You don't seem astonished," she said reproachfully.

"Why should I be?" I asked.

"Please turn your eyes toward the water. Suppose a Thermosaurus should look out of the waves!"

"Well," said I, "in that case the pleasure would be mutual."

She frowned, and bit her upper lip.

"Do you know what a Thermosaurus is?" she asked.

"If I am to guess," said I, "I guess it's a jellyfish."

"It's that big, ugly, horrible creature that I showed you in the shed!" cried Daisy impatiently.

"Eh!" I stammered.

"Not papier-maché either," she continued excitedly; "it's a real one."

This was pleasant news. I glanced instinctively at my rifle and then at the ocean.

"Well," said I at last, "it strikes me that you and I resemble a pair of Andromedas waiting to be swallowed. This rifle won't stop a beast, a live beast, like that Nibelungen dragon of yours."

"Yes, it will," she said; "it's not an ordinary rifle."

Then, for the first time, I noticed, just below the magazine, a cylindrical attachment that was strange to me.

"Now, if you will watch the sea very carefully, and will promise not to look at me," said Daisy, "I will try to explain."

She did not wait for me to promise, but went on eagerly, a sparkle of excitement in her blue eyes:

"You know, of all the fossil remains of the great bat-like and lizard-like creatures that inhabited the earth ages and ages ago, the bones of the gigantic saurians are the most interesting. I think they used to splash about the water and fly over the land during the Carboniferous period; anyway, it doesn't matter. Of course, you have seen pictures of reconstructed creatures such as the Ichthyosaurus, the Plesiosaurus, the Anthracosaurus, and the Thermosaurus?"

I nodded, trying to keep my eyes from hers.

"And you know that the remains of the Thermosaurus were first discovered and reconstructed by papa?"

"Yes," said I. There was no use in saying no.

"I am glad you do. Now, papa has proved that this creature lived entirely in the Gulf Stream, emerging for occasional flights across an ocean or two. Can you imagine how he proved it?"

"No," said I, resolutely pointing my nose at the ocean.

"He proved it by a minute examination of the microscopical shells found among the ribs of the Thermosaurus. These shells contained little creatures that live only in the warm waters of the Gulf Stream. They were the food of the Thermosaurus."

"It was rather slender rations for a thing like that, wasn't it? Did he ever swallow bigger food—er—men?"

"Oh, yes. Tons of fossil bones from prehistoric men are also found in the interior of the Thermosaurus."

"Then," said I, "you, at least, had better go back to Captain McPeek's——"

"Please turn around; don't be so foolish. I didn't say there was a *live* Thermosaurus in the water, did I?"

"Isn't there?"

"Why, no!"

My relief was genuine, but I thought of the rifle and looked suspiciously out to sea.

"What's the Winchester for?" I asked.

"Listen, and I will explain. Papa has found out—how, I do not exactly understand—that there is in the waters of the Gulf Stream the body of a Thermosaurus. The creature must have been alive within a year or so. The impenetrable scale armour that covers its body has, as far as papa knows, prevented its disintegration. We know that it is there still, or was there within a few months. Papa has reports and sworn depositions from steamer captains and seamen from a dozen different vessels, all corroborating each other in essential details. These stories, of course, get into the newspapers —sea-serpent stories—but papa knows that they confirm his theory that the huge body of this reptile is swinging along somewhere on the Gulf Stream."

She opened her sunshade and held it over her. I noticed that she deigned to give me the benefit of about one eighth of it.

"Your duty with that rifle is this: If we are fortunate enough to see the body of the Thermosaurus come floating by, you are to take good aim and fire—fire rapidly every bullet in the magazine; then reload and fire again, and reload and fire as long as you have any cartridges left."

"A self-feeding Maxim is what I should

have," I said with gentle sarcasm. "Well, and suppose I make a sieve of this big lizard?"

"Do you see these rings in the sand?" she asked.

Sure enough, somebody had driven heavy piles deep into the sand all around us, and to the tops of these piles were attached steel rings, half buried under the spear grass. We sat almost exactly in the centre of a circle of these rings.

"The reason is this," said Daisy: "every bullet in your cartridges is steel-tipped and armour-piercing. To the base of each bullet is attached a thin wire of pallium. Pallium is that new metal, a thread of which, drawn out into finest wire, will hold a ton of iron suspended. Every bullet is fitted with minute coils of miles of this wire. When the bullet leaves the rifle it spins out this wire as a shot from a life-saver's mortar spins out and carries the life line to a wrecked ship. The end of each coil of wire is attached to that cylinder under the magazine of your rifle. As soon as the shell is automatically ejected this wire flies out also. A bit of scarlet tape is fixed to the end, so that it will be easy to pick up. There is also a snap clasp on the end, and this clasp fits those rings that you see in the sand. Now, when you begin firing, it is my duty to run and pick up the wire ends and attach them to the rings. Then, you see, we have the body of the Thermosaurus full of bullets, every bullet anchored to the shore by tiny wires, each of which could easily hold a ton's strain."

I looked at her in amazement.

"Then," she added calmly, "we have captured the Thermosaurus."

"Your father," said I at length, "must have spent years of labour over this preparation."

"It is the work of a lifetime," she said simply.

My face, I suppose, showed my misgivings.

"It must not fail," she added.

"But—but we are nowhere near the Gulf Stream," I ventured.

Her face brightened, and she frankly held the sunshade over us both.

"Ah, you don't know," she said, "what else papa has discovered. Would you believe that he has found a loop in the Gulf Stream— a genuine loop—that swings in here just outside of the breakers below? It is true! Everybody on Long Island knows that there is a warm current off the coast, but nobody imagined it was merely a sort of backwater from the Gulf Stream that formed a great circular mill-race around the cone of a subterranean volcano, and rejoined the Gulf Stream off Cape Albatross. But it is! That is why papa bought a yacht three years ago and sailed about for two years so mysteriously. Oh, I did want to go with him so much!"

"This," said I, "is most astonishing."

She leaned enthusiastically toward me, her lovely face aglow.

"Isn't it?" she said; "and to think that you and papa and I are the only people in the whole world who know this!"

To be included in such a triology was very delightful.

"Papa is writing the whole thing—I mean about the currents. He also has in preparation sixteen volumes on the Thermosaurus. He said this morning that he was going to ask you to write the story first for some scientific magazine. He is certain that Professor Bruce Stoddard, of Columbia, will write the pamphlets necessary. This will give papa time to attend to the sixteen-volume work, which he expects to finish in three years."

"Let us first," said I, laughing, "catch our Thermosaurus."

"We must not fail," she said wistfully.

"We shall not fail," I said, "for I promise to sit on this sand hill as long as I live—until a Thermosaurus appears—if that is your wish, Miss Holroyd."

Our eyes met for an instant. She did not chide me, either, for not looking at the ocean. Her eyes were bluer, anyway.

"I suppose," she said, bending her head

and absently pouring sand between her fingers
—" I suppose you think me a blue-stocking, or
something odious? "

" Not exactly," I said. There was an em-
phasis in my voice that made her colour. After
a moment she laid the sunshade down, still
open.

" May I hold it? " I asked.

She nodded almost imperceptibly.

The ocean had turned a deep marine blue,
verging on purple, that heralded a scorching
afternoon. The wind died away; the odour of
cedar and sweet bay hung heavy in the air.

In the sand at our feet an iridescent flower
beetle crawled, its metallic green and blue wings
burning like a spark. Great gnats, with filmy,
glittering wings, danced aimlessly above the
young golden-rod; burnished crickets, inquisi-
tive, timid, ran from under chips of driftwood,
waved their antennæ at us, and ran back again,
One by one the marbled tiger beetles tumbled
at our feet, dazed from the exertion of an aërial
flight, then scrambled and ran a little way, or
darted into the wire grass, where great brilliant
spiders eyed them askance from their gossamer
hammocks.

Far out at sea the white gulls floated and
drifted on the water, or sailed up into the air
to flap lazily for a moment and settle back
among the waves. Strings of black surf ducks
passed, their strong wings tipping the surface

of the water; single wandering coots whirled from the breakers into lonely flight toward the horizon.

We lay and watched the little ring-necks running along the water's edge, now backing away from the incoming tide, now boldly wading after the undertow. The harmony of silence, the deep perfume, the mystery of waiting for that something that all await—what is it? love? death? or only the miracle of another morrow?—troubled me with vague restfulness. As sunlight casts shadows, happiness, too, throws a shadow, and the shadow is sadness.

And so the morning wore away until Freda came with a cool-looking hamper. Then delicious cold fowl and lettuce sandwiches and champagne cup set our tongues wagging as only very young tongues can wag. Daisy went back with Freda after luncheon, leaving me a case of cigars, with a bantering smile. I dozed, half awake, keeping a partly closed eye on the ocean, where a faint gray streak showed plainly amid the azure water all around. That was the Gulf Stream loop.

About four o'clock Frisby appeared with a bamboo shelter tent, for which I was unaffectedly grateful.

After he had erected it over me he stopped to chat a bit, but the conversation bored me, for he could talk of nothing but bill-posting.

"You wouldn't ruin the landscape here, would you?" I asked.

"Ruin it!" repeated Frisby nervously. "It's ruined now; there ain't a place to stick a bill."

"The snipe stick bills—in the sand," I said flippantly.

There was no humour about Frisby. "Do they?" he asked.

I moved with a certain impatience.

"Bills," said Frisby, "give spice an' variety to Nature. They break the monotony of the everlastin' green and what-you-may-call-its."

I glared at him.

"Bills," he continued, "are not easy to stick, lemme tell you, sir. Sign paintin's a soft snap when it comes to bill-stickin'. Now, I guess I've stuck more bills in New York State than ennybody."

"Have you?" I said angrily.

"Yes, siree! I always pick out the purtiest spots—kinder filled chuck full of woods and brooks and things; then I h'ist my paste-pot onto a rock, and I slather that rock with gum, and whoop she goes!"

"Whoop what goes?"

"The bill. I paste her onto the rock, with one swipe of the brush for the edges and a back-handed swipe for the finish—except when a bill is folded in two halves."

"And what do you do then?" I asked, disgusted.

"Swipe twice," said Frisby with enthusiasm.

"And you don't think it injures the landscape?"

"Injures it!" he exclaimed, convinced that I was attempting to joke.

I looked wearily out to sea. He also looked at the water and sighed sentimentally.

"Floatin' buoys with bills onto 'em is a idea of mine," he observed. "That damn ocean is monotonous, ain't it?"

I don't know what I might have done to Frisby—the rifle was so convenient—if his mean yellow dog had not waddled up at this juncture.

"Hi, Dəvy, sic 'em!" said Frisby, expectorating upon a clamshell and hurling it seaward. The cur watched the flight of the shell apathetically, then squatted in the sand and looked at his master.

"Kinder lost his spirit," said Frisby, "ain't he? I once stuck a bill onto Davy, an' it come off, an' the paste sorter sickened him. He was hell on rats—once!"

After a moment or two Frisby took himself off, whistling cheerfully to Davy, who followed him when he was ready. The rifle burned in my fingers.

It was nearly six o'clock when the professor

appeared, spade on shoulder, boots smeared with mud.

" Well," he said, " nothing to report, Dick, my boy? "

" Nothing, professor."

He wiped his shining face with his handkerchief and stared at the water.

" My calculations lead me to believe," he said, " that our prize may be due any day now. This theory I base upon the result of the report from the last sea captain I saw. I can not understand why some of these captains did not take the carcass in tow. They all say that they tried, but that the body sank before they could come within half a mile. The truth is, probably, that they did not stir a foot from their course to examine the thing."

" Have you ever cruised about for it? " I ventured.

" For two years," he said grimly. " It's no use; it's accident when a ship falls in with it. One captain reports it a thousand miles from where the last skipper spoke it, and always in the Gulf Stream. They think it is a different specimen every time, and the papers are teeming with sea-serpent fol-de-rol."

" Are you sure," I asked, " that it will swing in to the coast on this Gulf Stream loop? "

" I think I may say that it is certain to do so. I experimented with a dead right whale. You may have heard of its coming ashore here last summer."

"I think I did," said I with a faint smile. The thing had poisoned the air for miles around.

"But," I continued, "suppose it comes in the night?"

He laughed.

"There I am lucky. Every night this month, and every day, too, the current of the loop runs inland so far that even a porpoise would strand for at least twelve hours. Longer than that I have not experimented with, but I know that the shore trend of the loop runs across a long spur of the submerged volcanic mountain, and that anything heavier than a porpoise would scrape the bottom and be carried so slowly that at least twelve hours must elapse before the carcass could float again into deep water. There are chances of its stranding indefinitely, too, but I don't care to take those chances. That is why I have stationed you here, Dick, my boy."

He glanced again at the water, smiling to himself.

"There is another question I want to ask," I said, "if you don't mind."

"Of course not!" he said warmly.

"What are you digging for?"

"Why, simply for exercise. The doctor told me I was killing myself with my sedentary habits, so I decided to dig. I don't know a better exercise. Do you?"

"I suppose not," I murmured, rather red in the face. I wondered whether he'd mention fossils.

"Did Daisy tell you why we are making our papier-maché Thermosaurus?" he asked.

I shook my head.

"We constructed that from measurements I took from the fossil remains of the Thermosaurus in the Metropolitan Museum. Professor Bruce Stoddard made the drawings. We set it up here, all ready to receive the skin of the carcass that I am expecting."

We had started toward home, walking slowly across the darkening dunes, shoulder to shoulder. The sand was deep, and walking was not easy.

"I wish," said I at last, "that I knew why Miss Holroyd asked me not to walk on the beach. It's much less fatiguing."

"That," said the professor, "is a matter that I intend to discuss with you to-night." He spoke gravely, almost sadly. I felt that something of unparalleled importance was soon to be revealed. So I kept very quiet, watching the ocean out of the corners of my eyes.

IV.

Dinner was ended. Daisy Holroyd lighted her father's pipe for him, and insisted on my smoking as much as I pleased. Then she sat down, and folded her hands like a good little girl, waiting for her father to make the revelation which I felt in my bones must be something out of the ordinary.

The professor smoked for a while, gazing meditatively at his daughter; then, fixing his gray eyes on me, he said:

" Have you ever heard of the kree—that Australian bird, half parrot, half hawk, that destroys so many sheep in New South Wales? "

I nodded.

" The kree kills a sheep by alighting on its back and tearing away the flesh with its hooked beak until a vital part is reached. You know that? Well, it has been discovered that the kree had prehistoric prototypes. These birds were enormous creatures, who preyed upon mammoths and mastodons, and even upon the great saurians. It has been conclusively proved that a few saurians have been killed by the ancestors of the kree, but the favourite food of these birds was undoubtedly the Thermosaurus. It is believed that the birds attacked the eyes of the Thermosaurus, and when, as was its habit, the mammoth creature turned on its back to claw them, they fell upon the thinner scales of its stomach armour and finally killed it. This, of course, is a theory, but we have almost absolute proofs of its correctness. Now, these two birds are known among scientists as the ekaf-bird and the ool-yllik. The names are Australian, in which country most of their remains have been unearthed. They lived during the Carboniferous period. Now it is not generally known, but the fact is, that in 1801 Captain Ransom, of the British exploring vessel Gull, purchased from the natives of Tasmania the skin of an ekaf-bird that could not have been killed more than twenty-four hours previous to its sale. I saw this skin in the British Museum. It was labelled "unknown bird, probably extinct." It took me exactly a week to satisfy myself that it was actually the skin of an ekaf-bird. But that is not all, Dick, my boy," continued the professor excitedly. "In 1854, Admiral Stuart, of our own navy, saw the carcass of a strange gigantic bird floating along the southern coast of Australia. Sharks were after it, and, before a boat could be lowered, these miserable fish got it. But the good old admiral secured a few feathers and sent them to the Smithsonian. I saw them. They were not even labelled, but I knew that they were feathers from the ekaf-bird or its near relative, the ool-yllik."

I had grown so interested that I had leaned far across the table. Daisy, too, bent forward.

It was only when the professor paused for a moment that I noticed how close together our heads were—Daisy's and mine. I don't think she realized it. She did not move.

"Now comes the important part of this long discourse," said the professor, smiling at our eagerness. "Ever since the carcass of our derelict Thermosaurus was first noticed, every captain who has seen it has also reported the presence of one or more gigantic birds in the neighbourhood. These birds, at a great distance, appeared to be hovering over the carcass, but on the approach of a vessel they disappeared. Even in midocean they were observed. When I heard about it I was puzzled. A month later I was satisfied that neither the ekaf-bird nor the ool-yllik was extinct. Last Monday I knew that I was right. I found forty-eight distinct impressions of the huge seven-toed claw of the ekaf-bird on the beach here at Pine Inlet. You may imagine my excitement. I succeeded in digging up enough wet sand around one of these impressions to preserve its form. I managed to get it into a soap box, and now it is there in my shop. The tide rose too rapidly for me to save the other footprints."

I shuddered at the possibility of a clumsy misstep on my part obliterating the impression of an ool-yllik.

"That is the reason that my daughter warned you off the beach," he said mildly.

"Hanging would have been too good for the vandal who destroyed such priceless prizes!" I cried out in self-reproach.

Daisy Holroyd turned a flushed face to mine, and impulsively laid her hand on my sleeve.

"How could you know?" she said.

"It's all right now," said her father, emphasizing each word with a gentle tap of his pipe-bowl on the table edge; don't be hard on yourself, Dick, my boy. You'll do yeoman's service yet."

It was nearly midnight, and still we chatted on about the Thermosaurus, the ekaf-bird, and the ool-yllik, eagerly discussing the probability of the great reptile's carcass being in the vicinity. That alone seemed to explain the presence of these prehistoric birds at Pine Inlet.

"Do they ever attack human beings?" I asked.

The professor looked startled.

"Gracious!" he exclaimed, "I never thought of that. And Daisy running about out of doors! Dear me! it takes a scientist to be an unnatural parent!"

His alarm was half real, half assumed; but all the same, he glanced gravely at us both, shaking his handsome head, absorbed in thought. Daisy herself looked a little doubtful. As for me, my sensations were distinctly queer.

"It is true," said the professor, frowning

at the wall, " that human remains have been found associated with the bones of the ekaf-bird—I don't know how intimately. It is a matter to be taken into most serious considera-tion."

" The problem can be solved," said I, " in several ways. One is, to keep Miss Holroyd in the house———"

" I shall not stay in! " cried Daisy indig-nantly.

We all laughed, and her father assured her that she should not be abused.

" Even if I did stay in," she said, " one of these birds might alight on Master Dick."

She looked saucily at me as she spoke, but turned crimson when her father observed quietly, " You don't seem to think of me, Daisy."

" Of course I do," she said, getting up and putting both arms around her father's neck; " but Dick—as—as you call him—is so helpless and timid."

My blissful smile froze on my lips.

" Timid! " I repeated.

She came back to the table, making me a mocking reverence.

" Do you think I am to be laughed at with impunity? " she said.

" What are your other plans, Dick, my boy? " asked the professor.—" Daisy, let him alone, you little tease! "

"One is, to haul a lot of cast-iron boilers along the dunes," I said. "If these birds come when the carcass floats in, and if they seem disposed to trouble us, we could crawl into the boilers and be safe."

"Why, that is really brilliant!" cried Daisy.

"Be quiet, my child! Dick, the plan is sound and sensible and perfectly practical. McPeek and Frisby shall go for a dozen loads of boilers to-morrow."

"It will spoil the beauty of the landscape," said Daisy, with a taunting nod to me.

"And Frisby will probably attempt to cover them with bill-posters," I added, laughing.

"That," said Daisy, "I shall prevent, even at the cost of my life." And she stood up, looking very determined.

"Children, children," protested the professor, "go to bed—you bother me."

Then I turned deliberately to Miss Holroyd.

"Good-night, Daisy," I said.

"Good-night, Dick," she said, very gently.

v.

The week passed quickly for me, leaving but few definite impressions. As I look back to it now I can see the long stretch of beach burning in the fierce sunlight, the endless meadows, with the glimmer of water in the distance, the dunes, the twisted cedars, the leagues of scintillating ocean, rocking, rocking, always rocking. In the starlit nights the curlew came in from the sand-bars by twos and threes; I could hear their faint call as I lay in bed thinking. All day long the little ring-necks whistled from the shore. The plover answered them from distant lonely inland pools. The great white gulls drifted like feathers upon the sea.

One morning, toward the end of the week, I, strolling along the dunes, came upon Frisby. He was bill-posting. I caught him red-handed.

"This," said I, "must stop. Do you understand, Mr. Frisby?"

He stepped back from his work, laying his head on one side, considering first me, then the bill that he had pasted on one of our big boilers.

"Don't like the colour?" he asked. "It goes well on them boilers."

"Colour! No, I don't like the colour either. Can't you understand that there are some people in the world who object to seeing patent-medicine advertisements scattered over a landscape?"

"Hey?" he said perplexed.

"Will you kindly remove that advertisement?" I persisted.

"Too late," said Frisby; "it's sot."

I was too disgusted to speak, but my disgust turned to anger when I perceived that, as far as the eye could reach, our boilers, lying from three to four hundred feet apart, were ablaze with yellow and red posters, extolling the "Eureka Liver Pill Company."

"It don't cost 'em nothin'," said Frisby cheerfully; "I done it fur the fun of it. Purty, ain't it?"

"They are Professor Holroyd's boilers," I said, subduing a desire to beat Frisby with my telescope. "Wait until Miss Holroyd sees this work."

"Don't she like yeller and red?" he demanded anxiously.

"You'll find out," said I.

Frisby gaped at his handiwork and then at his yellow dog. After a moment he mechanically spat on a clamshell and requested Davy to "sic" it.

"Can't you comprehend that you have ruined our pleasure in the landscape?" I asked more mildly.

"I've got some green bills," said Frisby; "I kin stick 'em over the yeller ones——"

"Confound it!" said I, "it isn't the colour!"

"Then," observed Frisby, "you don't like them pills. I've got some bills of the 'Cropper Bicycle,' and a few of 'Bagley, the Gents' Tailor——'"

"Frisby," said I, "use them all—paste the

whole collection over your dog and yourself—
then walk off the cliff."

He sullenly unfolded a green poster,
swabbed the boiler with paste, laid the upper
section of the bill upon it, and plastered the
whole bill down with a thwack of his brush.
As I walked away I heard him muttering.

Next day Daisy was so horrified that I promised to give Frisby an ultimatum. I found
him with Freda, gazing sentimentally at his
work, and I sent him back to the shop in a
hurry, telling Freda at the same time that she
could spend her leisure in providing Mr. Frisby
with sand, soap, and a scrubbing brush. Then
I walked on to my post of observation.

I watched until sunset. Daisy came with
her father to hear my report, but there was
nothing to tell, and we three walked slowly
back to the house.

In the evenings the professor worked on
his volumes, the click of his type-writer sound-
ing faintly behind his closed door. Daisy and
I played chess sometimes; sometimes we played
hearts. I don't remember that we ever finished
a game of either—we talked too much.

Our discussions covered every topic of interest: we argued upon politics; we skimmed
over literature and music; we settled interna-
tional differences; we spoke vaguely of human
brotherhood. I say we slighted no subject of
interest—I am wrong; we never spoke of love.

Now, love is a matter of interest to ten people out of ten. Why it was that it did not appear to interest us is as interesting a question as love itself. We were young, alert, enthusiastic, inquiring. We eagerly absorbed theories concerning any curious phenomena in Nature, as intellectual cocktails to stimulate discussion. And yet we did not discuss love. I do not say that we avoided it. No; the subject was too completely ignored for even that. And yet we found it very difficult to pass an hour separated. The professor noticed this, and laughed at us. We were not even embarrassed.

Sunday passed in pious contemplation of the ocean. Daisy read a little in her prayer-book, and the professor threw a cloth over his typewriter and strolled up and down the sands. He may have been lost in devout abstraction; he may have been looking for footprints. As for me, my mind was very serene, and I was more than happy. Daisy read to me a little for my soul's sake, and the professor came up and said something cheerful. He also examined the magazine of my Winchester.

That night, too, Daisy took her guitar to the sands and sang one or two Armenian hymns. Unlike us, the Armenians do not take their pleasures sadly. One of their pleasures is evidently religion.

The big moon came up over the dunes and

stared at the sea until the surface of every wave trembled with radiance. A sudden stillness fell across the world; the wind died out; the foam ran noiselessly across the beach; the cricket's rune was stilled.

I leaned back, dropping one hand upon the sand. It touched another hand, soft and cool.

After a while the other hand moved slightly, and I found that my own had closed above it. Presently one finger stirred a little—only a little—for our fingers were interlocked.

On the shore the foam-froth bubbled and winked and glimmered in the moonlight. A star fell from the zenith, showering the night with incandescent dust.

If our fingers lay interlaced beside us, her eyes were calm and serene as always, wide open, fixed upon the depths of a dark sky. And when her father rose and spoke to us, she did not withdraw her hand.

" Is it late? " she asked dreamily.

" It is midnight, little daughter."

I stood up, still holding her hand, and aided her to rise. And when, at the door, I said good-night, she turned and looked at me for a little while in silence, then passed into her room slowly, with head still turned toward me.

All night long I dreamed of her; and when the east whitened, I sprang up, the thunder of the ocean in my ears, the strong sea wind blowing into the open window.

"She is asleep," I thought, and I leaned from the window and peered out into the east.

The sea called to me, tossing its thousand arms; the soaring gulls, dipping, rising, wheeling above the sand-bar, screamed and clamoured for a playmate. I slipped into my bathing suit, dropped from the window upon the soft sand, and in a moment had plunged head foremost into the surf, swimming beneath the waves toward the open sea.

Under the tossing ocean the voice of the waters was in my ears—a low, sweet voice, intimate, mysterious. Through singing foam and broad, green, glassy depths, by whispering sandy channels atrail with seaweed, and on, on, out into the vague, cool sea, I sped, rising to the top, sinking, gliding. Then at last I flung myself out of water, hands raised, and the clamour of the gulls filled my ears.

As I lay, breathing fast, drifting on the sea, far out beyond the gulls I saw a flash of white, and an arm was lifted, signalling me.

"Daisy!" I called.

A clear hail came across the water, distinct on the sea wind, and at the same instant we raised our hands and moved toward each other.

How we laughed as we met in the sea! The

white dawn came up out of the depths, the zenith turned to rose and ashes.

And with the dawn came the wind—a great sea wind, fresh, aromatic, that hurled our voices back into our throats and lifted the sheeted spray above our heads. Every wave, crowned with mist, caught us in a cool embrace, cradled us, and slipped away, only to leave us to another wave, higher, stronger, crested with opalescent glory, breathing incense.

We turned together up the coast, swimming lightly side by side, but our words were caught up by the winds and whirled into the sky.

We looked up at the driving clouds; we looked out upon the pallid waste of waters; but it was into each other's eyes we looked, wondering, wistful, questioning the reason of sky and sea. And there in each other's eyes we read the mystery, and we knew that earth and sky and sea were created for us alone.

Drifting on by distant sands and dunes, her white fingers touching mine, we spoke, keying our tones to the wind's vast harmony. And we spoke of love.

Gray and wide as the limitless span of the sky and the sea, the winds gathered from the world's ends to bear us on; but they were not familiar winds; for now, along the coast, the breakers curled and showed a million fangs, and the ocean stirred to its depths, uneasy, ominous, and the menace of its murmur drew us closer as we moved.

Where the dull thunder and the tossing spray warned us from sunken reefs, we heard the harsh challenges of gulls; where the pallid surf twisted in yellow coils of spume above the bar, the singing sands murmured of treachery and secrets of lost souls agasp in the throes of silent undertows.

But there was a little stretch of beach glimmering through the mountains of water, and toward this we turned, side by side. Around us the water grew warmer; the breath of the following waves moistened our cheeks; the water itself grew gray and strange about us.

"We have come too far," I said; but she only answered: "Faster, faster! I am afraid!" The water was almost hot now; its aromatic odour filled our lungs.

"The Gulf loop!" I muttered. "Daisy, shall I help you?"

"No. Swim—close by me! Oh-h! Dick——"

Her startled cry was echoed by another—a shrill scream, unutterably horrible—and a great bird flapped from the beach, splashing and beating its pinions across the water with a thundering noise.

Out across the waves it blundered, rising little by little from the water, and now, to my horror, I saw another monstrous bird swing-

ing in the air above it, squealing as it turned
on its vast wings. Before I could speak we
touched the beach, and I half lifted her to the
shore.

"Quick!" I repeated. "We must not
wait."

Her eyes were dark with fear, but she rested
a hand on my shoulder, and we crept up among
the dune grasses and sank down by the point of
sand where the rough shelter stood, surrounded
by the iron-ringed piles.

She lay there, breathing fast and deep,
dripping with spray. I had no power of speech
left, but when I rose wearily to my knees and
looked out upon the water my blood ran cold.
Above the ocean, on the breast of the roaring
wind, three enormous birds sailed, turning and
wheeling among each other; and below, drifting with the gray stream of the Gulf loop, a
colossal bulk lay half submerged—a gigantic
lizard, floating belly upward.

Then Daisy crept kneeling to my side and
touched me, trembling from head to foot.

"I know," I muttered. "I must run back
for the rifle."

"And—and leave me?"

I took her by the hand, and we dragged
ourselves through the wire grass to the open
end of a boiler lying in the sand.

She crept in on her hands and knees, and
called to me to follow.

"You are safe now," I cried. "I must go back for the rifle."

"The birds may—may attack you."

"If they do I can get into one of the other boilers," I said. "Daisy, you must not venture out until I come back. You won't, will you?"

"No-o," she whispered doubtfully.

"Then—good-by."

"Good-by," she answered, but her voice was very small and still.

"Good-by," I said again. I was kneeling at the mouth of the big iron tunnel; it was dark inside and I could not see her, but, before I was conscious of it, her arms were around my neck and we had kissed each other.

I don't remember how I went away. When I came to my proper senses I was swimming along the coast at full speed, and over my head wheeled one of the birds, screaming at every turn.

The intoxication of that innocent embrace, the close impress of her arms around my neck, gave me a strength and recklessness that neither fear nor fatigue could subdue. The bird above me did not even frighten me; I watched it over my shoulder, swimming strongly, with the tide now aiding me, now stemming my course; but I saw the shore passing quickly and my strength increased, and I shouted when I came in sight of the house, and scrambled up on the sand, dripping and excited. There was nobody in sight, and I gave a last glance up into the air where the bird wheeled, still screeching, and hastened into the house. Freda stared at me in amazement as I seized the rifle and shouted for the professor.

"He has just gone to town, with Captain McPeek in his wagon," stammered Freda.

"What!" I cried. "Does he know where his daughter is?"

"Miss Holroyd is asleep—not?" gasped Freda.

"Where's Frisby?" I cried impatiently.

"Yimmie?" quavered Freda.

"Yes, Jimmie; isn't there anybody here? Good heavens! where's that man in the shop?"

"He also iss gone," said Freda, shedding tears, "to buy papier-maché. Yimmie, he iss gone to post bills."

I waited to hear no more, but swung my rifle over my shoulder, and, hanging the cartridge belt across my chest, hurried out and up the beach. The bird was not in sight.

I had been running for perhaps a minute when, far up on the dunes, I saw a yellow dog rush madly through a clump of sweet bay, and at the same moment a bird soared past, rose, and hung hovering just above the thicket. Suddenly the bird swooped; there was a shriek and a yelp from the cur, but the bird gripped it in one claw and beat its wings upon the sand, striving to rise. Then I saw Frisby—paste, bucket, and brush raised—fall upon the bird, yelling lustily. The fierce creature relaxed its talons, and the dog rushed on, squeaking with terror. The bird turned on Frisby and sent him sprawling on his face, a sticky mass of paste and sand. But this did not end the struggle. The bird, croaking wildly, flew at the prostrate billposter, and the sand whirled into a pillar above its terrible wings. Scarcely knowing what I was about, I raised my rifle and fired twice. A horrid scream echoed each shot, and the bird rose heavily in a shower of sand; but two bullets were embedded in that mass of foul feathers, and I saw the wires and scarlet tape uncoiling on the sand at my feet. In an instant I seized them and passed the ends around a cedar tree, hooking the clasps tight. Then I cast one swift glance upward, where the bird wheeled screeching, anchored like a kite to the pallium wires; and I hurried on across the dunes, the shells cutting my feet, and the bushes tearing my wet swimming suit, until I dripped with blood from shoulder to ankle. Out in the ocean the carcass of the Thermosaurus floated, claws outspread, belly glistening in the gray light, and over him circled two birds. As I reached the shelter I knelt and fired into the mass of scales, and at my first shot a horrible thing occurred: the lizardlike head writhed, the slitted yellow eyes sliding open from the film that covered them. A shudder passed across the undulating body, the great scaled belly heaved, and one leg feebly clawed at the air.

The thing was still alive!

Crushing back the horror that almost paralyzed my hands, I planted shot after shot into the quivering reptile, while it writhed and clawed, striving to turn over and dive; and at each shot the black blood spurted in long, slim jets across the water. And now Daisy was at my side, pale and determined, swiftly clasping each tape-marked wire to the iron rings in the circle around us. Twice I filled the magazine from my belt, and twice I poured streams of steel-tipped bullets into the scaled mass, twisting and shuddering on the sea. Suddenly the birds steered toward us. I felt the wind from their vast wings. I saw the feathers erect, vibrating. I saw the spread claws outstretched, and I struck furiously at them, crying to Daisy to run into the iron shelter. Backing, swinging my clubbed rifle, I retreated, but I tripped across one of the taut pallium wires, and in an instant the hideous birds were on me, and the bone in my forearm snapped like a pipestem at a blow from their wings. Twice I struggled to my knees, blinded with blood, confused, almost fainting; then I fell again, rolling into the mouth of the iron boiler.

.   .   .   .

When I struggled back to consciousness
Daisy knelt silently beside me, while Captain
McPeek and Professor Holroyd bound up my
shattered arm, talking excitedly. The pain
made me faint and dizzy. I tried to speak and
could not. At last they got me to my feet and
into the wagon, and Daisy came, too, and
crouched beside me, wrapped in oilskins to her
eyes. Fatigue, lack of food, and excitement
had combined with wounds and broken bones
to extinguish the last atom of strength in my
body; but my mind was clear enough to understand that the trouble was over and the
Thermosaurus safe.

I heard McPeek say that one of the birds
that I had anchored to a cedar tree had torn
loose from the bullets and winged its way
heavily out to sea. The professor answered:
" Yes, the ekaf-bird; the others were ool-ylliks.
I'd have given my right arm to have secured
them." Then for a time I heard no more; but
the jolting of the wagon over the dunes roused
me to keenest pain, and I held out my right
hand to Daisy. She clasped it in both of hers,
and kissed it again and again.

. . . .

There is little more to add, I think. Professor Bruce Stoddard has edited this story
carefully. His own scientific pamphlet will be
published soon, to be followed by Professor Holroyd's sixteen volumes. In a few days the

stuffed and mounted Thermosaurus will be placed on free public exhibition in the arena of Madison Square Garden, the only building in the city large enough to contain the body of this immense winged reptile.

When my arm came out of splints, Daisy and I —— But really that has nothing to do with a detailed scientific description of the Thermosaurus, which, I think, I shall add as an appendix to the book. If you do not find it there it will be because Daisy and I have very little time to write about Thermosaurians.

But what I really want to tell you about is the extraordinary adventures of Captain Mc-Peek and Frisby—how they produced a specimen of Samia Cynthia that dwarfed a hundred of Attacus Atlas, and how the American line steamer St. Louis fouled the thing with her screw.

The more I think of it the more determined I am to tell it to you. It will be difficult to prevent me. And that is not fiction either.

ENVOI.

ENVOI.

I.

When shadows pass across the grass
And April breezes stir the sedge,
Along the brimming river's edge
  I trail my line for silver trout,
And smoke, and dream of you, my lass,
  And wonder why we two fell out,
  And how the deuce it came about.

II.

When swallows sheer the meadow-mere
And thickets thrill with thrushes' hymns,
Along the mill-pond's reedy rims
  I trail my line for shining dace;
But how can finny fishes cheer
  A fellow, if he find no grace
  In your sweet eyes and your dear face?

III.

Let thrushes wing their way and sing
Where cresses freshen pebbled nooks;
By silent rills and singing brooks
  I pass my way alone, alas!
With your dear name the woodlands ring—
  Your name is murmured by the grass,
  By earth, by air, all-where I pass.

IV.

The painted bream may swim the stream—
   I'll cast no line to-day, pardi !
In vain the river-ripples gleam,
   In vain the thrushes' minstrelsy.
Vain is the wind that whispers, "Lo !
Thy fish are waiting—Angler, go !"

V.

Will you forgive if I forgive ?
Life is too sad, I think, to live
Alone, and dream and smoke and fish ;
I'll say "Forgive" first—if you wish ?

VI.

For at that word, the Sorcery
Of Love shall change the earth and sky
To Paradise, with cherubim
Instead of birds on every limb.

VII.

Rivers shall sing our rhapsody ;
The vaulted forest, tree by tree,
High hung with tapestry, shall glow
With golden pillars all a-row.

VIII.

And down the gilded forest aisle
Shy throngs of violets shall smile
And kiss your feet from tree to tree
While blue-bells droop in courtesy.

IX.

And if the sun incarnadine
The clouds—green leaves shall be your screen ;

And if the clouds with jealousy
Should weep—we'll beg of some kind tree
A moment's hospitality.

X.

Good cheer is here, if you incline;
Moss-hidden springs shall bubble wine
While squirrels chuckle, rank on rank,
And strawberries from every bank
Shall blush to see how deep we drank.

XI.

Winds of the West shall cool our eyes
While every woodland creature tries
His voice a little, so that he
May know his notes more perfectly
When crickets start the symphony.

XII.

Through hazel glade and scented dell
Where brooklets ring a tinkling bell,
The forest orchestra shall swell,
Until the sun-soaked grasses ring
With crickets strumming string on string.

XIII.

Then, with your white hand daintily
Scarce touching mine, we'll leave our tree
And ramble slowly toward the West
Where our high castle's flaming crest,
Towering behind the setting sun,
Flings out its banners, one by one,
Signals of fire, that day is done.

XIV.

Deep in that palace we shall find
How blind we are, how blind ! how blind !
And how he'll laugh, who holds the key
To the great portal's mystery !
And how his joyous laugh will ring
When you and I shall bid him fling
The gates ajar for you and me !

XV.

Let shadows flee athwart the lea
When dark December strips the hedge
Along the icy river's edge;
  Yet, if you will forgive me, lass,
The world shall bloom like spring to me,
  Snow turn to dew upon the grass
  And fagots blossom where you pass.

XVI.

Swallows shall sheer the frozen mere,
Dead reeds along the mill-pond's rims
Shall thrill with summer-thrushes' hymns,
  While summer breezes blow apace,
If you will but forgive me, dear,
  And let me find a moment's grace,
  In your sweet eyes and your dear face.

                                           R. W. C.

THE END.